The Imposter King

(Book 2 of The Imposter Series)

By

Wendy Rathbone

**The Imposter King Copyright © 2018
by Wendy Rathbone and Eye Scry Publications**

**A publication by:
Eye Scry Publications**
www.eyescrypublications.com

TITLE: The Imposter King
Author: Wendy Rathbone
ISBN# 978-1-942415-24-4

Address all inquiries to the author at:
wendy@eyescrypublications.com

Acknowledgments

Also, a thousand thank yous to **Christina E. Pilz** for a wonderful beta-read of this novel.

And last but best of all, thank you to my partner **Della Van Hise** for help with formatting and uploading my books. I couldn't do this without you.

Chapter One

"Dare. Dare."

Dare loved it whenever Mal said his name. It didn't matter where or when, just that voice, low and smooth, pressing the air with that princely undertone.

Prince Malory was hot-headed, fiery. His body moved a lot, even when sleeping. He tended to be quick and terse to servants and guards, even to his own father. But when he spoke to Dare, or said his name, his voice changed. Every time. It softened. It contained a resonance of unchecked pleasure.

The way he said his name. The way he spoke to Dare. All day. Every day. It felt like seduction.

Of course seduction was a big part of their lives. Before, and now after their marriage, simply, they could not get enough of each other. Dare could get aroused just watching Mal breathe. Or walk. Or stoop to wipe mud from the top of his boot.

But that voice. When he turned it fully onto Dare, Dare's insides began to burn, sweet and searing, and without volition his mind began to plan where they might go in the next few free minutes away from duties to the realm. Where they might find a little privacy—a servant's closet, a bower in the walled gardens, the corner of a balcony no one ever used—so they could once again touch, press, join.

Right now, they occupied a lovely bower in the gardens. The scent of orchids and hyacinth surrounded them.

The late afternoon, all amber and muted—slid through the curving branches of the willow overhead. Dark ivy crawled up the brick walls. Bird-song and dulcet buzzing surrounded them.

Mal lay on an ornate, white-painted iron bench. It might have been uncomfortable for him, except the servants stocked these little alcoves with freshly laundered pillows every day. So his bare buttocks were cushioned on velvet stuffed with soft sheep's wool.

Dare leaned across the bench between Mal's legs, using his mouth to help cool the nearly constant and insistent fires of their adoration for each other.

Mal groaned. Dare smiled around the appendage that filled his mouth, and moved slowly up and down. He loved the salty tartness, the smooth rigidity.

It was always exquisite with Malory. There was no other word for it. This desire, this ardor, this lust. This love-making.

They burned this way all the time. He wasn't sure either of them would survive it.

His own cock nudged his trousers. It throbbed and demanded. Threatened to singe its way right through the material that encased it. He could feel dampness there. Urgency.

Malory's fingers petted Dare's hair, combing through the thick strands in a gentle massage.

A breeze blew in, fluttering leaves and petals and ruffles of up-raised white shirts. It brushed its coolness against flushed cheeks, bellies, and thighs. A willow's fronds curtained this particular bower, and the leaves undulated, giving off a green, fresh scent.

Mal said, "Dare. Dare."

So close. Dare reached up with his hand and cupped the drawn up balls, so tight but the skin soft as breath, the hairs fine as silk.

That was all it took. Malory arched up. Pulsed. Came.

Dare drank as if it were nectar. And indeed it was. The nectar of euphoria. Of the man he loved most in all the realms.

It took a while for Mal to be done. It seemed he always wanted more, more. But finally he pulled back, though his pretty cock was still hard. He shoved Dare down to the spill of pillows, pushing his shirt up. He ran his hands up and down Dare's chest. Next thing Dare knew, his trousers were pushed down to his calves. Mal caressed and licked his way to the prize.

He was so hard he wasn't going to last. He didn't care.

The mouth encased him, damp, burning, sucking.

He could not hold back the groans. "Unn, umph, Mal—
"

Mal let Dare's cock slide from his mouth. "Just a little more, that's all you need. Then you'll be fine."

Dare slammed the side of his head against the back of the bench, letting the curlicues of thick metal press his cheek. His eyes shut tight.

When Mal took him into his mouth, he sucked all the way down and Dare lost control, coming hard. This was his world at its very best. The reason for being. Not just the lovemaking, although that was good, but this intimacy. The sharing of himself in this precious way with Malory. That was all he wanted. How could he have ever thought there was anything more?

In these moments, he found his source and his prize all in one place. In the arms of his best friend, his lover, his husband.

Two princes. Once enemies. Both from different realms. Now they were sworn to each other, united, and through their combined strength it seemed as if nothing was out of their reach.

When coherency returned, Dare heard Mal saying, "So beautiful." Over and over.

"I love you." Dare reached up, and their mouths met, their arms wrapped about each other.

Mal's wild, blond hair tickled Dare's forehead and jaw. He hugged him tighter, wanting to stay this way forever. Their kisses were so full of life; certainly they would be enough to live on, along with their whispered endearments, hushed and pure against the backdrop of pearlescent light and sun-warmed skies. Their devotion was so fevered they need not worry about icy winters. They could melt right through them, roll in snow and rain and still not feel anything but the sizzle and blush of their sensual yearnings, their hearts melting together, fused as one.

But danger crouched. Always in the backs of their minds. For Dare was not a real prince. Not by blood. Not by anything, really, but marriage to a prince.

No one knew that, though. For he had played the role of Prince Darius from Brookfall so well that even when the real Darius had been alive, and everyone in Shastan believed that he was the Crown Prince, that he would inherit the realm of Brookfall.

Only Mal knew the truth. And Mal had vowed to protect the lie with his life.

Everyone here in Shastan had been a stranger to him when he'd first arrived. They didn't know, couldn't know that he had really been only the servant-companion to the real Prince Darius. A boy the real prince called "Footstool". They didn't know that Dare doubled for the prince at public functions, that the real prince, before he died, had been a troubled boy, depressed, a bully, a young man who panicked at the thought of stepping one foot outside castle walls, let alone meeting new people.

The secret of Dare's true origins hovered like a shadow over their bliss. Always there. A storm cloud waiting to burst, containing the rain of a poisoned elixir. A presence of danger made of desperation and fear and instinct for survival. It was real, this lie, like a person. And it always stood over them. Watching.

Dare pressed harder into the kiss. The sparks of it took away all that darkness. Mal obviously felt it, too. The edge of their shared deceit like a sharp threat that someday might wedge itself between them.

Their love kept them close. Their fear made them closer. Possibly it was why they stayed near to each other at all times, always touching. Why they slept entwined. Why Dare often woke with Mal spread out on top of him as if to ward off any harm that might come Dare's way.

Now they lay together on the bench, on the pillows, and the fire of passion tried to rise again.

Mal chuckled into their kiss, his response to the increase of heat.

Dare turned his head and buried his face in the crook of Mal's neck.

"We have meetings," Dare whispered.

"Fuck the meetings."

"Fuck the council?"

"Yeah, that, too."

"I'd be jealous," Dare said.

More chuckling.

Finally, they got themselves up. Just in time, too, for they could hear voices through the willow fronds coming closer.

Dare pulled up his trousers and tucked in his shirt. Mal was faster, already parting the fronds to see who was coming up the path before Dare was finished.

"Wait," Dare protested.

Mal turned to look him up and down. "What? You're dressed."

Dare patted down his wrinkles and stood straighter, peering over Mal's shoulder. He saw the queen coming up the trail with two of her guardsmen and a female companion.

"Don't let her see me," Dare whispered.

"Why the hell not? You're my legal husband. I'm allowed to be in a bower with you."

"She hates me."

"She doesn't."

"She does."

Mal grinned at him as Dare ran his hands over his own hair.

Dare said, "Do I look all right? Do I look normal, I mean, not like we've been doing what we—uh, have been doing?"

Mal reached out and brushed a finger over Dare's lips. "Well, you have a little bit of—"

Horrified, Dare pushed his hand away and started rubbing at his mouth.

"Just joking," Mal said. His white teeth flashed. His light brown eyes still radiated the thrill of their last minutes. There was no way the queen would remain ignorant of what they had been up to.

Mal walked onto the path. "Hello, Mother."

"Malory. The council is meeting just now. I thought you were there," said the queen, arching her eyebrows.

"Why aren't you there, Mother?"

"You know full well your father hates having me there"

Dare came out from between the willow fronds to stand at Mal's side. He faced the queen and bowed. "Your Highness."

Her perfect blond eyebrows frowned. She was where Mal had gotten his coloring from. Her hair and skin was even lighter than his. She looked like an ice queen from a fairytale about Snowland.

Dare shivered.

"Ah, now I see why you're late." Her petite nose wrinkled. "My son, have I failed to teach you your royal duties come first?"

Not intimidated for a single moment, Mal said, "I have a royal duty to my husband, too."

"Yes, you do. In the proper place. At the proper time."

Mal put his hands behind his back and leaned in to kiss her cheek. "You didn't teach me that part."

The pale pink of her cheeks darkened.

Dare felt his own face flame. It was always like this. Mal so easy and nonchalant. Making everyone around him flustered and yet feeling important at the same time.

It was a wonder the entire realm wasn't in love with him.

But he was Dare's husband now. And the thought made him want to yell it from the tops of the castle towers. *I LOVE PRINCE MALORY!*

The queen pretended nothing was amiss, that she had not blushed, that she did not love her only son very very much. She said, "You're late! The two of you! Off with you to the council chambers now!"

Mal turned and pulled Dare to his side. Arm in arm, they headed for the garden entrance at a quick pace.

Chapter Two

The interior hall leading to the council chamber glowed soft white, polished to a muted shine. The sconces gave off amber haloes. Two unicorn statues carved of ancient cherry wood guarded either side of the doors. The unicorn was the crest of Shastan, and was painted on every shield, banner and war cloak.

These unicorns were reared up on their hind legs, their fore-legs frozen in mid-smack at the air. Their manes looked wind-blown, tossed back, curling upward; their faces contorted, angry, or perhaps scared.

Dare liked unicorns, but these two statues always unnerved him.

Mal strode through the double oak doors as if he already ruled. Dare followed.

Inside, the long, rectangular table was surrounded by men sitting in wooden chairs.

Among them, Dare saw King Millard who was Malory's father, Lord Blackwell, the king's right hand, Lord Mistiff—whom everyone called Mist—who oversaw the outlands of Shastan, as well as others whose provinces were part of Shastan but still ruled under independent governments.

Lastly, his eyes met the dark green-gray gaze of Lord Stix, the king's own dungeon-master, and someone Dare knew all too well from his two-day and one night incarceration in the dingy prison. It had been the rainy season when he'd stayed there for one night, and none too pleasant. Add to that the whipping Dare had received, and Stix's never-ending penchant for philosophical lecturing on the state of the soul and the true definitions of freedom, and Dare allowed himself a small glare at the man.

Mal said, "We were unexpectedly detained by the queen."

Dare glanced at the king, who scowled a bit. He knew they both spent every spare moment alone together.

No one dared say a word.

Mal sauntered to his place near the king and took his seat. Dare sat in the empty chair that was nearest to the prince. That chair stood just around the edge of the head of the table, and faced Lord Mist.

"We haven't missed anything, have we?" Mal boldly asked.

"In fact," said the king, "you have. But nothing to concern your spoiled head with."

"Indeed?" Mal quipped.

Lord Stix sat one chair down from Lord Mist, and appeared neat, tidy and handsome as ever with his dark features. Dare watched him out the corner of his eye. Despite his torrid journey to the dungeon, he could not help but respect the man, who always looked sharp, fastidious and even sad. His deep brown hair was pulled neatly back in a tail. His smooth cheeks and slender hands bespoke of a youth not quite extinguished. Stix was the apologetic sadist of the realm, and it would have all seemed like a big joke if the man was not so good at his job.

Dare could see the man looking unabashedly at him, though Dare kept his own gaze steady on the parchment underneath Mist's flattened palms on the tabletop.

King Millard said, "But now that you are both here, Prince Darius, there is a matter I'd like to bring up with you."

"Of course, Your Highness." A twinge of nerves burned up and down Dare's arms.

"It has been several months now since you arrived. Since then, we have sent many couriers to Brookfall with messages from myself on behalf of this realm, and from you,

Prince Darius. All have gone unanswered. We have been waiting a long time. Though your father has made no further moves or declarations of war against us, we are impatient with the lack of communication. It is an insult."

"I have told you all I know," Dare said. "My father was not mentally well when I left. I have no more idea what is happening in Brookfall right now than you do, aside from rumors and whatever your spies have reported."

"Yes, I know. But further insight is needed at this time. The situation between our realms remains unsolved. It is a great cause of anxiety among this council and all our peoples."

"I am not sure what more I can tell you. I understand the insult to this country," said Dare. "I do not approve, but I cannot force my father to answer my letters."

"No. You cannot."

"What do you expect him to do about it?" Mal interjected.

"I think it's time for Prince Darius to make a visit back to his homeland. To see his father. To appeal to him."

Dare felt all the blood drain from his face. Beside his father, Mal straightened.

"He can't do that!" Mal protested.

King Millard turned to his son. "Of course he can. And you can go with him as our emissary."

"No, it's a terrible idea." His words came fast, almost dismissive.

"Do not take that tone with me."

In silent horror, Dare watched father and son argue. Though they did it all the time, Dare never got used to it.

"I will take this tone! The king of Brookfall left Dare for dead. He didn't care if his so-called beloved son was executed for his own crimes against our realm. He tossed our ambassadors out in the night where they were attacked. He's already turned his back on Prince Darius. And all of us!"

The lines in King Millard's rugged features deepened. There was a tinge of warm bronze in his eyes, but no softness.

"I will send the best warrior guardsmen with you. If you have to fight your way to the castle and face him at sword point, so be it."

"You can't be serious!"

"I am."

"But Father, that is an act of war. And sending Dare in now—he could be seen as a traitor and beheaded for treason!"

The voice that Dare loved so much, that caressed him in the night with sweet compliments and arduous demands, turned dark and rough.

"Let us ask Prince Darius's opinion on the matter, then," said the king.

Dare gulped. He barely knew the king of Brookfall even though he'd been raised with the real Prince Darius his whole life. Whenever Dare saw the king at public functions, doubling as the prince, the king kept himself apart, rarely spoke to him, and showed no affection at all.

In Castle Brookfall, all the closed meetings the real Prince Darius had with his father had been off-limits to Dare.

Those meetings had always made Darius darker and angrier afterward. Made him quick-tempered on the prowl to push around the servants and bully Dare

The times the king came to the prince's rooms to check up on him were rare and short-lived. He usually chastised Darius for his behavior and ordered Dare to look after him better as defined by his companion duties.

More recently, he'd come cold and still aching from his whipping in the dungeons here in Shastan to be judged by King Millard. The moment he'd decided to plead for his life with an idea of unification, begging the king to reinstate the past offer of marriage between the realms to ensure future peace.

That was the moment he'd seen the swans flying, a portent for change. From then on, everything *had* changed for him. He'd declared his love for the Shastan prince and Malory

14

had become his. He'd pledged fealty to Malory as well as his father and mother, the king and the queen.

Even now, his pledge held firm. He would do anything to uphold the peace between the realms. Anything except this. For if he returned home, his secret would be revealed. He was nobody. A mere servant. Not only would two realms suffer real war because of it, but he and Malory would be separated forever. Dare would be imprisoned for life, or executed. Either king would be within their rights to do so.

Dare inhaled. Exhaled loudly. Malory, beside his father, was all shades of gold in his white shirt, his chin held high. But in those honey eyes a glimmer of fear flawed his perfect visage.

"Prince Darius," the king prompted. "What is your perception of this plan?"

His voice came out thinner than he wished. Unsure. "I do not wish to return to Brookfall."

"That is not the question I asked."

"Father, let him talk."

"My father will not be happy to see me. He never was happy to see me even before I was brought here." *Before I was brought here and taken hostage. Kept as a bargaining tool. Sentenced to the dungeon.*

"What if a meeting was set at a neutral place? On grounds at the border of both our realms?"

"Not good enough!" Mal said. "He shouldn't have to go at all."

"Hush for a moment," King Millard said. "Prince Darius. What about a meeting between you and your father on neutral grounds, such as the Firestar Monastery at the foot of Blue Hill. It's right on the border."

"I—I—" Dare glanced at Mal whose eyes were wide and full.

"You would be protected by my best guardsmen. I would guarantee that."

"You can't guarantee his safety!" Mal yelled, standing in such rage that his chair slid back with a screech on the hard floor.

Before the king could reprimand Mal again, Dare said, voice low, "I don't know." He realized he sounded quite calm, but that was what tension did to his voice. It took it, froze it in his throat, and made it small or non-existent. "I don't know that my father would even agree to such a meeting."

"I agree. He's responded to none of our other messages," Mal said.

"But we've never sent a message offering to allow him to see his son. This may be the one message that makes him respond."

Dare stared at Mal, who shook his head almost imperceptibly. Dare saw such caring there in his gaze, along with a strong protective love, and just that small gesture sent a ray of warmth through Dare's chest. Mal would do everything he could to protect him. Everything and anything.

But that scared Dare most of all because he never wanted to see Mal's position compromised, or any harm come to him. If Dare were ever to be compromised for his secret, he would make sure Mal did not go down with him. If it meant sacrificing himself and their relationship, he would do it.

The worst part about that, though—Mal would never hesitate to do the same for Dare.

Dare said, "My father might respond to having a meeting with me. I don't know."

"It all may be a moot point," said the king. "But it is a strategy for the betterment of life between our two realms. We must send the message and hope he responds."

The other council members spoke their opinions, speculating on the wording of the message, and whether or not the neutral place of the monastery the king suggested was the most suitable one.

Dare's mind was a blur. He could not comprehend a word. He could only look helplessly at Mal and no longer

16

wonder *if* their world would be destroyed. Now it was only a matter of *when*.

When Dare heard Stix's voice speak up, he saw Mal narrow his eyebrows. Mal's mouth curled, unfriendly.

Despite the whipping Stix had given him, Dare didn't hate him as much as Mal did. He focused all his attention on the man.

"It seems to me," Stix said, "that Prince Darius has become an asset to be kept alive at all cost. He will become king of Brookfall one day. To risk that future for a meeting now, well, it might construed as hasty."

"Hmm." King Millard leaned forward, hands on the tabletop. "Interesting opinion. He is the crown prince. He will inherit unless his father disowns him. There has been no official rumor to that effect, but it could already be in place. In which case, Brookfall would never welcome him as their king even if the throne is his rightful place."

"My father has no other living heirs," Dare said. "He is a very proud man. He would hate the idea of a line other than his own blood to take over the reign of Brookfall."

"He had a brother. What about that prince's offspring?"

Dare shook his head, recalling a time when he was around twelve years of age.

Darius had mentioned the castle had received word of the death of his uncle. Darius had laughed in his cruel and jesting way, stating haughtily that his uncle was not getting a royal funeral because his father had banished him. When Dare had tried to show any sympathy, Darius had said, *What do I care about a stupid uncle I never met anyway?*

"They were estranged. I know of no offspring," Dare replied.

"So the chance that he would disown you, even knowing you are friendly with the enemy, is slim." The king waited.

Dare swallowed. His throat was dry and no servants had yet brought wine.

"Name is most important to him." Dare's throat felt scratchy. "More, even, than love. He has no love for me, or very little, but for the name. The name is what he wants to live on. Even if his estranged brother had offspring, he'd never consider them as true heirs."

"You have all given me a lot to ponder. I shall think on this for the night and we will meet in council with my final decision tomorrow," King Millard said.

Mal leaned toward the king, forcing him to look at him, their faces inches apart. "Father, you can't think on it for one minute. Dare said his father values the name above all else. He will not disown his own son. Dare will become king. But if you send Dare and his father into a forced meeting, who knows what might happen?"

"This is my decision to make," the king said, meeting his son's gaze with equal force. "Tomorrow the council will meet again. That is my pronouncement."

"But Father—"

The king stood, glaring down at Mal. "Are you going to sit there and argue with me all day?"

Mal stood. "I will if it is to keep you from doing something stupid."

Dare gasped. The rest of the council took it in stride, used to the father and son tirades. But it always made Dare uneasy. Even though the real Prince Darius fought with his own father, it was always behind closed doors, in private meetings. Never in public. And never at a council meeting, since the real Prince Darius had never been allowed to attend one.

"This meeting is over for now," King Millard said, turning away from his son. "If council members have topics they wish to bring up, it can wait until tomorrow."

Mal's hands fisted at his waist. His body was tight, held in at the shoulders. He kept his chin up, never taking his gaze off his father as the king left the council room.

Dare came up alongside him, placing a hand on his back, barely touching.

"He'll see that you're right," Dare said. "He will."

Mal turned, voice soft, pitched just for Dare. "I'm not so sure."

Chapter Three

Twilight made the walls ashen where its dim light flowed through the high windows of the baths. The pools became ethereal and silvery this time of day. Little slaps of water echoed through the damp air, and despite the scents of lavender oil and sandalwood soap, and the promise of warm water, chills prickled Dare's skin.

Malory was all bustling energy and deep flame as he disrobed. Dare loved how Mal's body moved as if barely contained within his skin, his spirit fluid and flickering no matter his mood: angry, sad, aroused.

Though Mal was a prince, and somewhat spoiled, he was so much the opposite of the real Prince Darius Dare had grown up with and served. Everything about Darius had been dark and hateful and oppressive. He'd been Dare's tormentor, dominating Dare's every waking hour with his disgust for life and his tantrum-like fears.

Malory was like the sun after a long storm. He strode through the palace at Shastan as if he already owned it. He'd distrusted Dare at first, but he'd gotten to know him. Curiosity was one of Mal's many attractive traits. And he was one of the most honest men Dare had ever met.

Thus, keeping their lie intact seemed destructive to that beautiful soul. Dare regretted it every day, but had no solutions. He'd been ordered to play the role of Prince Darius with Darius's own dying words.

It had seemed the only way out, the only way to save his life that fateful day he'd been taken by Shastan guardsmen. But now, if he was forced to meet the king of Brookfall, the only possible outcome would be disaster on so many different levels he could not count the pain.

"It can't happen. It just can't happen." Mal had been repeating that sentence over and over since before they'd arrived at the baths.

They were in the royal section of the baths, where there was some privacy. The large pool was edged on one side by a white wall, on the other by a scaffolding of red curtains. The back of the pool opened to a little area with a fountain sprinkling into a small pool barely ankle-deep. The front held the bench, facing the shallow end and the steps, and on either side of the bench stood two large pots with fake trees, their leaves made of dyed green leather, the branches formed from carved wood. They were quite beautiful works of art.

Dare folded his shirt and placed it on a flat, wooden bench. He undid his trousers and let them slip to the floor. He kicked his boots away and turned toward the water, quite aware that Malory was watching him, liking the feeling of being wanted.

He waded into the warm water and immediately his tense body began to relax. When Dare looked back, Mal was naked, facing away from him, taking his time folding his trousers.

The strain in Mal's shoulders was obvious by the taut muscles, and the way he held himself, always tall, always regal, but elbows pulled in now, neck stiff.

Finally, Mal turned. Dare could not contain his smile at the beauty of him.

Mal kept his eyes forward and descended the steps. Dare pushed himself through the water, going deeper, but still facing him. That chiseled chest, flat stomach, strong thighs. The water slowly came up his body to encase Mal. When it reached his genitals, that beautiful cock floated upward a bit, so pretty and perfect that Dare wanted him again.

His body heated in the warm water. The pleasure of looking at Mal washed over him, an intense longing. This. This was everything. Malory. The palace. Being a prince now. He could not lose this.

"Dare."

There it was. That voice. Saying his name. Like it was a prayer.

Dare came forward until they two of them were only inches apart.

Mal said, "My father is so stubborn."

"Yes."

"If I have to disguise myself and run away with you, I will."

It pleased Dare to hear that Mal would go that far to save him. But of course Dare would never allow that. Still, the fantasy posed a sort of thrill.

"You'd do that?"

Mal reached out. "For you. Anything."

Dare moved into his embrace. Liquid sloshed between them, gentle and intimate, as if the water itself were fond of them.

Their bodies met, slippery now. Nuzzling together. Flame to flame. Growing heat. Hearts quickening.

The embrace, although sensual, was more. As if they wanted to climb into each other, grab hold and stay forever. It was desperation. Hunger. Possession.

"I will not see you destroyed by this, Mal," Dare whispered.

Mal's chest heaved with a small but bitter laugh. "Me? Destroyed? I'm invincible." He pressed his cheek into the top of Dare's shoulder.

Dare held him tight as the water circled and sought and glimmered in endless craving about them, a demanding third lover in its own right pressing against their bodies.

Dare could feel Mal's erection against his thigh. It was so nice to be wanted like this all the time. So wonderful. His body always filled to the brim with the excitement of longing and the joy of having the object of that longing at his side and in his arms every day and every night.

His embrace tightened. Mal's hands slipped up and down his back. His hair tickled Dare's cheek. Finally, Mal turned to face him and pressed his lips to Dare's, gentle at first, feeling the texture and the curve of them. Dare pulled back a little, teasing him with the kiss before he opened his mouth to Mal's, tasting the wine of him, growing dizzy.

Mal's hand cupped the back of his neck. And Dare was lost.

This was normal, right? They were young. This happened. This thing where they couldn't get enough of each other.

They moved back up the steps and sat naked on the blue tiled pool-edge, hands going everywhere, sliding up and down muscles and ribs and shoulder blades. Fingers gently tangling in each other's hair. Letting out occasional low sounds like moans and small growls of pleasure.

Mal picked up a bottle of olive oil and it slipped from his fingers and plinked into the water, landing on the first shallow step. Dare made a grab for it. Mal teasingly slapped his hand away, grabbed the bottle and turned Dare to face away from him.

Dare knelt on the first step and rested his chest on the lip of the pool, waiting for those knowing, gentle hands. They caressed him lovingly, rough palms, strong fingers, and then one oiled finger delved deeply into him. He pressed back onto it with a hiss. His cock was so hard it hurt. Just as he had that thought, another hand snaked around his hips and caressed him there, milking, and Dare gave a long sigh of delight.

The finger that opened him left to be replaced by Mal's erection. He wanted it so much he had to grit his teeth to keep from keening. "Please," he managed. "I want it now."

"You do?" Mal asked. "Now?"

The head of his cock pressed against his opening. It would be tight at first, maybe sting a bit, but only for a second. Then he would feel Mal inside him and he would want to move and he would want Mal to move and he would wish with all his heart that this might never end.

"Do it!"

Mal pushed in easier than Dare thought it would be, well-oiled, ready. Dare was so aroused that he felt no pain. The slide of Mal into his body felt like warmth on a cold day, or a soothing balm to an open ache. His eyes grew damp, the moisture there sweet, making the sconce-light molten.

He put his forehead down on his folded arms and bucked his hips back.

Mal gave a short grunt and began to make love to him with earnest, smooth, gentle thrusts.

It was the best. Thing. Ever.

As Mal moved inside him, he stroked Dare's cock, palming him just right, letting his thumb whisper against the damp head to tease and taunt. Dare's body grew hotter. After a short while, the feeling of Mal inside him seemed to melt his insides. He gripped with his internal muscles, wanting to take that feeling deeper. His entire body felt on the verge of coming apart.

Mal's forehead pressed into the back of Dare's neck. He felt a kiss on his shoulder, a dampness, a quick bite.

"Please," Dare groaned.

Mal's free arm snaked around him, holding him closer. It was as if they merged into one being. He wanted to turn. He wanted to face his lover, grab hold, meld lips, pull him into him and make him stay that way, softly rocking, for minutes, for hours, forever.

But this way was good, too. Front to back. Dare pushed back hard with his hips. Mal stroked his cock faster, his other arm curved tight against his ribs. Dare couldn't breathe. He didn't care. He didn't need to breathe. If he breathed, he might lose this moment. He wanted it extended. He wanted all of time to freeze.

Ah, those quickening, short thrusts. The way Mal bit him again, right at the crook of his neck. The feel of Mal's flat chest against the broadness of his own back. And that heat. Like an inferno between them, as if they might burn up and together rise to the skies, ash mixing with the stars.

The build of pleasure inside him rushed up, an exalted form of being, and he could no longer keep it down, keep himself together. He let out his held breath all at once and his cock twitched beautifully, pulsing hard. He felt his balls clench and a gush of liquid rushed through his shaft. He came hard, flowing onto Mal's stroking hand, spattering the edge of the pool. For several long moments he went blind and the world was a white, fragmented shatter of light rays and crystals and gleaming white, featureless landscapes. The whiteness itself careened. He was part of something else now. Something other.

Distantly, he heard Mal call his name in that lovely way he did that aroused Dare so much, and that set him off again. Cock pulsing.

He did not want to come down from this white state of being. He wanted to exist there always. But then he felt Mal's arms around him, holding him, still calling. And he couldn't resist the man. "Dare. Dare."

He wanted to live with him. Be with him. Through Mal he could revisit this place of sacred passion over and over. Mal was his conduit to purity of soul, ecstasy. Love.

A few short months ago, he would never have had a single thought to dream of a life like this, a life with one he loved so fiercely.

He felt the essence of Mal on him, in him, and knew Mal had gone to that place as well, the swirling, twirling whiteness of being.

Mal had turned him on the edge, bringing him down into the inch of water that coated the first step.

Dare reached up and pulled him to him, holding on.

"You're trembling so hard," Mal said, brushing his lips with a kiss.

Dare sighed, smiling so wide it hurt. "Kiss me again."

Mal's kisses: Like waves of sunlight, gulps of the finest wine, sweetness unmeasured. Their tongues danced.

Finally, Dare pulled away, gasping for breath.

"I think I'm drowning in you."

Mal chuckled. "As long as you're not drowning in the pool."

"I want you all the time."

"Good." A smug expression lifted Mal's lips. His chin came up. "Good," he said a second time.

Dare laughed in the afterglow as his lover—his husband—pulled him into the water for a soak.

The water seemed to blend with his skin. The sweet flowery scent of it filled him up.

Mal ran his hands up and down Dare's arms. His wrist caught on Dare's silver bracelet. "Your mother's bracelet." He fingered the bangle, catching it, pulling Dare closer. "Have you ever taken it off?"

"Not since I was five."

"You pay her a great tribute."

"She was a servant. I have no idea where she got a piece of jewelry like this. But I do remember her giving it to me. I didn't understand at the time that she was dying."

"She must have loved you very much."

Dare nodded. He could barely remember her, but Mal's words made him smile.

When they tired, breathless, they both emerged dripping and took turns rubbing each other dry with the soft towels put out clean every day by the servants.

Dare took his time drying Mal, loving his body, kneeling to wipe every inch of skin, lingering on his thighs, placing a kiss upon the side of his beautiful cock which made Mal hiss. He ran the towel with reverence over the strong buttocks and firm back.

When it was his turn, Mal treated him as if he were a precious jewel he was polishing. He said, breathing on Dare's cock, "I'll suck you."

"Again?" But even Dare he spoke, his cock hardened.

Without another word, Mal took it into his mouth, softly suckling, gentle, knowing he was still sensitive from just making love. But Dare wanted him so much that at his age coming often wasn't a problem. Just the touch of Mal's tongue against his sensitive skin sent him reeling.

Mal brushed a palm over his balls, lightly cupping, and strengthened the pull from his mouth. Sucking always made Dare hard fast. He clenched his fingers to fists, trying to make it last, but Mal was too good and Dare was too in love. Little tongue flicks on the tip and the mouth going down his shaft, sucking harder, faster, then repeating, and it wasn't long before he felt the surge of ecstasy. It was slightly less intense this time, but still fantastic.

He sat down as Mal leaned in and kissed him. Dare could taste himself on Mal's lips.

Mal spread Dare's knees and toweled him clean, so loving, and then said, "Sit and turn. I want to put oil on your scars."

Dare turned, still trembling from his second orgasm, and let Mal rub lavender oil into the whip marks from Stix in the Shastan dungeon. He had older scars from when Darius as well. None of them hurt, but Mal was disturbed by them and said he always wanted to make sure the scars were oiled so they didn't harden and pain Dare when they pulled with the natural movements of his body. To be so well taken care of was a luxury Dare had never known before Mal.

When Mal was done, he turned and kissed him. Dare leaned back and ran his fingers over Mal's blond bramble of soft hair. "Thank you."

They kissed again. This time Mal's cock took notice, and Dare watched its pink head push free of the foreskin, the tiny hole glistening with need. Simply, they could not get enough of each other.

Mouth watering for the sweetness of his lover, he bent his head between Mal's legs and fed.

27

Chapter Four

A thudding knock came at the royal chamber door, banging over and over. The sound echoed in the corners, pushing into Dare's sleep, making him jerk awake.

Dare raised his head from the pillow, blinking to clear his vision from the hazy dreams he'd been having of Mal holding him, touching him.

Mal, hair in his face, sat bolt upright.

"What?"

The door opened. Outside, as if too shy to enter, stood two guards.

"Your Highness." The smaller one spoke.

"Yes?" Mal asked. "Get on with it. What is it? It's very early still, barely dawn. Why are you knocking?"

"There's been a message received."

"What are you talking about?"

The guard said, "A message just came from the king of Brookfall. King Millard wants everyone in the council chambers at once."

Dare's heart began to knock in his chest. He sat very still, covers at his waist, chest naked to the air, and to the rosy light that had begun to turn the room and all its shadows dusky purple.

It had been over a week since King Millard had made his decision at the second council meeting to send a new message to the king of Brookfall stating that he would allow him to see his son. Mal had been enraged. Dare used every ounce of patience and love to calm his quick tempers since then.

"Before breakfast?" Mal asked, stretching lazily, pretending nonchalance. In truth, Dare knew he was as nervous as he was over recent events.

"Yes, sir. Now. Dress quickly. The king is waiting."

"But—"

The chamber door shut on Mal's words.

Mal turned to Dare. "Fuck."

"I know. It sounds urgent. I wonder what—"

"Shhh." Mal reached for him. "We're not going to panic yet. I'm just pissed."

Dare's own nerves made his body suddenly feel light and queasy. He shook his head. "If he wants a meeting, I don't know—"

Mal kissed him to shut him up. He leaned back, brushing fingers to Dare's cheek.

"Shh. You've been so cool and calm all week, settling my tempers. Now it's my turn. Don't worry. You know I'll make sure everything is okay. Just. Well. Fuck."

"I know." But Dare wondered how Mal might think, in the face of all of it, he could make anything better. "I'm so sorry. This is all my fault. Everything—it's my doing. Now it's all coming to a head. I should never have—"

Mal put his fingers to Dare's lips, pressing.

"Shh. You are not to blame. Never. I've been pissed about those two council meetings all week, but today I'm going to take a stronger stand. It's our lives at stake. But honestly, I don't see the point to life if I can't make love you first thing in the morning." He forced a chuckle. "Tell me I'm right."

Dare knew Mal was trying to distract him, make him smile.

Mal reached between Dare's legs and touched him, just a brush, soft and inviting.

"Oh," Dare said in an out-rush of air. One hand clutched Mal's upper arm, the naked skin and hard muscle smooth against his palm.

Dare was usually hard in the mornings, as was Mal, and they sometimes did it twice before breakfast. But now Dare's cock did not respond. He couldn't focus. All he could think about now was if the king of Brookfall saw him, everything would be over. He'd tell everyone Dare was just a servant. And he would have him executed.

"But I—I—" Dare's eyes filled.

"Shh." Mal pulled him to his chest. "I'll take care of you. I promise. Forever."

Dare nodded against him, nose pressing Mal's shoulder.

Mal said, "We'll get dressed and go see my father. No matter what is so urgent, or what the message says about you going to Brookfall, it's not the end. Nothing can happen today. Nothing will be fully decided, all right?"

But Dare knew that King Millard had a streak of defiance against Brookfall, and he loved to take opposing positions to any of Prince Malory's opinions.

Mal jumped from the edge of the bed and dragged Dare out with him. They both stood shivering in the early dawn. Mal reached out and rang the bell for their dressing servants, but before they arrived, both men were already mostly fully clothed. After all, the guards had said to hurry.

The servants helped with lacing tall boots, hair, jewelry, and shaving. They were ready within a short span. The sun had barely crested the horizon.

When they entered the council chambers the king had not yet arrived. The oil lamps glowered orange to gold as another servant turned them to their highest settings.

Mal and Dare took their usual seats. A servant poured them tea and served warm biscuits smothered in honey, which neither Dare nor Mal touched.

Finally, more council members arrived, including Stix who always gave Dare long looks whenever they were in the same room. They had never spoken privately since the time Dare had spent in the royal dungeon, but Dare was aware that Stix gave him special attention. It made him nervous. He was sure he had given nothing away about his secret while in the dungeon, but he couldn't be sure. Had he slipped up in something he'd said, a word choice, or how he conducted

30

himself? He'd grown up around a prince. He'd played the part of a prince. There wasn't much he didn't know about *being* a prince, but maybe somehow Stix suspected something was off.

Whatever it was, Stix made Dare's skin crawl more than from a memory of being whipped by him.

When King Millard arrived, everyone stood. He wore his purple robe belted at the waist. As the room was cold from the morning air he also wore a short, white fur cloak.

He made no preliminaries, but started in with the reason for the emergency meeting.

"Early this morning," he began, "two messengers from Brookfall rode into our courtyard accompanied by our guard. They were carrying gifts and a message from the king of Brookfall. The message held an answer to my invitation last week to the king to meet with his son Prince Darius at the border."

"Father, this can't—" Malory started to stand.

King Millard held his hand up to silence his son. "I have convened this council to tell you that the king had accepted my invitation. And more."

Dare's heard sank. His skin went cold. He watched as Malory's chest rose with a deep breath. He was poised, ready to argue as always.

"What *more*?" Mal demanded.

King Millard ignored him, turning his gaze to Dare. It remained there for a few tense moments, unwavering. "Prince Darius. Your father has finally ransomed you."

Malory started to jump up again.

Other voices in the room rose in question.

King Millard ignored them. "The message says that there will be no war between our realms if Prince Darius is returned alive and unharmed. He also sent four bags of gold, three as payment for our hardship in caring for the prince, and one to pay for the prince's journey home. The gold is worth far more than any amount spent so far on the prince."

"But this is an insult," shouted Mal. "There is no ransom demand. There has been no expenditure past the first few weeks Dare was here. Dare is my husband!"

"I understand that, son," the king said.

"But why now, after all the unanswered scrolls, even messages from his own son?" Mal asked.

"May I speak?" Dare asked.

The king nodded.

"It is apparent," Dare said, "that word has gotten back to Brookfall that I married Prince Malory. My father was against it. In fact, he was insulted by the suggestion that I marry the prince." He turned to look at the king. "He wants me back if the marriage is annulled, no doubt."

The king nodded. "Yes. And that is not part of my bargain. I want you to know, Dare, that you are part of my family now and I will honor that."

Mal made a disgusted noise, fists pressed tight to the table-top.

"Patience, my son," the king said quietly. He glanced back to Dare. "The question now is if we send you to meet him and reassure him of your well-being, will you be able to convince him to recognize this marriage? Will peace between our realms be kept?"

"Recognition of the marriage as valid or not makes no difference. If you don't send him, peace will surely fail," Stix interrupted quietly.

Much as he didn't like it, Dare knew Stix was right.

Dare turned to look at Malory. The golden prince's face was pale with an almost gray sheen. He looked as if he'd just eaten poison.

What were they going to do? The king of Brookfall wanted to not only see him, but keep him. The gold was buying Dare's way back to Brookfall forever. There was no way around it. His secret would be known to all then, and the realms would fall apart. Dare would be imprisoned or beheaded.

32

Dare's hand began to shake. There was no way out of this now.

Mal said, "The ransom is an insult. Dare is not a prisoner. We tell him no. We tell him his son has found a home here and is safe. And that Dare doesn't want to see him and wants to stay as a guarantee for peace now and on into the future."

"Why ever would you suggest that, son?" the king asked.

Mal took a few breaths. He looked almost panicked and Dare worried that everyone here in the council chamber would see their deception.

"Because," Mal finally answered. "Because we can't trust him. Dare has told us this. Over and over. The man is a madman. And besides, Dare doesn't want to see him again. We all should be respecting that."

"I appreciate your opinion, son, but the truth of the matter is with a ransom technically met—unlimited peace with no stipulations—as well as payment for good faith, this cannot be so simply ignored."

"You cannot send Dare back to that madman. Not even for one day." Mal leaned over the table, palms flat on its surface. "I have a say, too. He is my husband. I have promised in a ceremony of highest honor to protect him, to keep him from all harm, to stand by him always. You cannot send him back!"

"Which is why," the king said, "you will, of course, accompany him on this journey which will be a meeting only. You will go as my emissary, of course. And it will be your task to keep Dare safe at all cost. I would never part you from him. I will not turn Dare over to him forever. You are newlyweds. And I am neither a thoughtless king nor a cruel father."

"But—"

King Millard held his hand up again. "That's my decision. It's final. The details will be worked out within the next week."

33

Mal stood. "A week? That's not long enough to—"

"That's my final decision," the king said, getting up, no longer looking at his son. "That will be all. This emergency session of the council is over."

With a swish of his long robe, the king strode from the room to his attached private office chamber. The rest of the council members rose, chattering excitedly among themselves.

Dare sat frozen in his chair. It was as if all the air in the chamber had leaked out, leaving nothing left but dust motes and cold dawn forcing its way through the now open door. Nothing but the sconces flickering like deadly eyes, watching, suspicious, knowing there were secrets soon to unravel and such drama to behold.

Blood rushed in his ears. A loud hum. The sides of the chamber darkened. He could see only through a blur, his eyes focusing on Stix who was the last council member to leave.

Stix was staring at him, eyebrows narrowed. Stix was reading his mind. He had that talent. It was why he was a dungeon master, and a sadist. He saw people's quirks and flaws; no weakness escaped his vision. He could see that Dare was more than just apprehensive about going home. He was terrified.

Dare met Stix's eyes. The blood rushed louder. Something blocked his view. Dare tried to shake it off but it wouldn't move. Something grabbed his shoulder. A voice came from far away, through the low hum. A beloved voice.

"Dare."

The hand on Dare's shoulder gripped tight, shaking him.

He looked up into Mal's strong face. "I can't do this," Dare whispered.

As if from another room, Mal's voice came to him. "I'm going to figure this out. I promise you. I will be with you every step of the way."

All week Dare had leaned heavily against the hope that the mad king of Brookfall would never answer King Millard's message, that as with all the former messages, it would be ignored. Now he had to face the inevitable reality that his secret would now be unraveled by all.

"I can't. I don't see how I can go home. Ever."

"Come with me," Mal urged.

Dare could not move or breathe. His whispers of protest had taken whatever breath had been left in his lungs.

"Dare." Mal put one hand under his arm, coaxing him up.

Dare gave no response. Already he was falling away into nothingness,
his entire identity counterfeit, a sham. He was no one. He was nothing.

"Dare, get up."

He felt himself lifted into gentle arms. Was Stix still at the door witnessing this? No, he couldn't be. Mal knew Dare wouldn't want that man seeing him so vulnerable.

Still, Dare's heart hammered in his chest as he came up onto wobbly legs and leaned into Mal's chest.

"I can't," Dare whispered again.

"Come on. I've got you. I'm taking you back to our rooms. It'll be all right, I promise. I have some ideas."

But Dare knew this was something Mal couldn't promise. Their secret was going to come out. There was no way to keep it no matter what sorts of plans Mal made. Maybe they could plead with the king and he'd understand, make a new plan to deal with Brookfall? Maybe they could go away together for awhile?

But he knew none of his thoughts were reasonable.

On that fateful day the real Prince Darius died in his arms, he should have been honest with the guards, taken his punishment right then and there even if it meant sure death. For this was certainly far more torturous. And worse, it put Mal's life in danger as well.

What a selfish man I am, Dare thought. *A selfish horrible man.*

He heard soft words but could not make out what they were. Strong arms led him from the now-hazy council chambers. Mal. Mal was with him. Protecting him. Caring for him. For now.

But all Dare could think was: *It's over.*

He did not remember climbing the stairs at all, or when Mal sat him on the plush couch before the roaring hearth. The next thing he knew, an array of trays had been laid out on the low, wooden table before the couch. They contained sliced honeyed pears, grapes still on the vine, hot rolls dripping in butter, scrambled eggs, bite-sized squares of cheese, steaming cups of tea.

Mal was talking. Dare finally heard some words. "We're going to sit and eat. And talk. And we're going to figure some things out. Dare. Please look at me. You have to trust me. I am not going to let anything happen to you."

Dare looked up into the striking tawny eyes. Mal's hair was as wild as ever, framing his face in part ringlets, part tangles. And so golden. He was like a lion in many ways. Even his demeanor. Pacing. Always thinking. Arguing. Scheming. Mal. He was the best thing that had ever happened to Dare.

"I trust you," Dare finally said.

Chapter Five

"I look enough like the real Prince Darius," Dare began, "that the people of the realm will believe I am him. I attended public events as him for most of our teen years. They would easily know me to be him. But the ones who will know me on sight—the ones we can't fool—are the king's advisors, the servants to the king and, most importantly, the king himself. I cannot return to Brookfall!"

They had been sharing hare-brained plans for the past half hour.

They sat on Mal's plush couch facing the flickering hearth. In moderate temperatures, the fire was allowed to go down to mostly embers with occasional hard oak wood thrown on to burn slow and steady. The air smelled already of summer.

Mal had one hand to his face, rubbing his left eye. "Or then—I know, I know—your secret will be revealed."

"Well, of course it will!" Dare frowned. "We could disguise ourselves and run, live somehow—but that wouldn't be fair to you."

"That's a last resort, but one I would consider. And fairness be damned." Mal looked up through his fingers which were now worrying the tangles at his forehead. "I just want to be with you. I'd give it all up in a heartbeat."

Dare shook his head. "I wouldn't let you." He shut his eyes tight until white sparks danced across the insides of his eyelids.

"Then we amend the plan for the meeting. We do not go to Brookfall. We go to the border only and no one sees you but the king."

"How is that a better amendment to the plan? The king is our biggest problem!"

"You can convince him, somehow, that you represent Prince Darius's best interests. Maybe he won't care that his son won't see him. He doesn't know his son is dead. We'll keep that secret to our graves."

Dare opened his eyes. The room's shadows wavered darkly. "When traveling, he's always surrounded by his guard. And his advisors travel with him. It will be impossible that others won't recognize me and see a ploy."

"He was always using ploys," Mal said. "Your king was allowing his son to use you as an impersonator. We'll think up a good reason why you must see him and only him alone. And we won't stay long. At least not long enough for anyone else to catch a glimpse of you. We'll only stay long enough to convince him his son is well and does not wish to see him. That you and he alone survived that trip to the chalet. We'll do everything we can to keep the peace."

They left that plan aside for the moment as they discussed alternatives throughout the morning.

"We could say my face was injured and I can't show it in public."

"Veil you?" Mal asked.

"Yes."

"It would look bad on Shastan. They might say we harmed you and start a war over that. But it's still an interesting idea."

A shudder ran up and down Dare's body.

Mal leaned forward, putting his hand on Dare's knee. "I will never leave your side."

"I am afraid it will all be over. And just when I've gotten so much—you, a place where I feel happy, an identity that isn't mine but that I've molded to be mine. But I've done wrong, so now I'll be punished for it. It's the way of things, right?" His eyes stung. Deep inside his belly, a cold chill began. "It's the way the world balances itself out."

Mal moved closer to him. "It's not my way." He put his arm over Dare's shoulders, a welcome warm weight. "Bad things happen to good people. Good things happen to bad people. You're not going to be punished because we will figure this out."

Dare wanted to believe him, to lean into Mal's powerful assurances and know the outcome for them would result in endless seasons of shared affinity and love, and an old age still wrapped in each other's arms.

Dare bowed his head. "What if—what would your father say—or do if he found out?"

"If we confided in him?"

"Yes." Dare started to nod, unsure. "Maybe we could make him understand. To prevent a war. And then he would protect us and refuse to send us to the border."

Mal sighed, then bent and pressed his cheek to the side of Dare's head. "My father is not a bad man. But I don't know how he would take the truth of you knowing I knew all along."

"You're right," Dare interrupted. "It was a terrible idea. Too much time has passed. If I reveal myself to him now, the betrayal is even worse. It's treason, it's—"

"Stop." Mal lifted his fingers to Dare's lips, a feathery brush. "We won't talk of that.

Dare shivered again, despite the fire and the warm air. "But it is treason," he whispered. "The worst crime against the crown short of regicide."

"We are saving two kingdoms from the atrocities of war with this secret. How can saving a kingdom—two kingdoms—be treason?" Mal asked.

"You and I see it that way," Dare said. "But others won't. People get strange thrills out of seeing their icons fall."

"Which is why they won't find out. And when it's time to see your father the king, we will make an arrangement."

"I don't see how. No matter what, he'll want war. If I am veiled from injury and won't show my face, he'll want war." He began to pace. "If tell him I am still doing Darius's bidding by impersonating him, he'll want war against the country he perceives brainwashed his son. It will be his revenge. And he won't stop until he gets it. I know that man. He's as unreasonable as Darius was. Paranoid and angry and cold." He paused, staring upward. Remembering. "Darius was his father's son through and through. I could deal with Darius, even understand him sometimes, but the way he saw the world... every shadow lurking was a personal enemy. No one could be trusted. Nothing was bright or fun or contained any hope. The king himself was not overtly cruel, but he was cold, and never happy since the queen died. It got worse over time. He saw threats everywhere and to protect himself and his kingdom he would wage war without a second thought. The only thing left to him is his name and he would risk a whole kingdom, and die to protect that name, and to avenge his son."

"But you said he did not love Darius."

"I never saw much love between them, but he was a symbol. The name was everything. Brookfall. The King of Brookfall and his son Prince Darius. They have the same name, you know. But the king did not like using it. He just wanted to be called "the king". The name alone, the symbol of that, of maintaining that line, was still everything to him, though. It may be why he was offended when the offer of marriage between you and his son became known to him. He saw an heirless future, and usurpers at the gate."

"Hmm." Mal leaned closer to Dare.

Dare wanted to embrace him, but his muscles wouldn't obey. He was stiff from shock and fear. "I feel sick," Dare said.

"We can use that."

"What?"

"What you just said," Mal explained. "The carrying on of the name. That. It's so important to him, that maybe he will accept you so the name can continue."

Dare shook his head and crossed his arms tighter over his chest. "He won't. I'm not blood-related. We'll be walking into a death-trap. And then there will be war. It's hopeless."

He wanted to curl up, go back to bed, hide forever. It wasn't like him. He took on challenges well. He had put up with Darius and his cruelty his whole life, never arguing with him, always fixing his problems. And now, he had lived through an ambush, Darius dying in his arms, fever, and the dungeon. Even then, he'd not given up. But now everything felt tumbling toward an ending he could not prevent. A crash. A fall. The destruction of this beautiful and terrifying dream.

"Nothing is hopeless," Mal said.

Mal's arm curved around him. His face pressed against Dare's hair, lips caressing the edge of his ear.

But right now Dare could feel nothing but the cold spreading in a slow wave from his stomach to his heart.

Chapter Six

For the first time since they were married, Dare turned away from Mal in their marriage bed.

He felt horrible. Rotten for his secret and terrible about how it made him want to curl up, pull into himself, and hide away. Leaving Mal behind.

Mal pressed up behind him but lay still and undemanding. Dare could feel his intense heat. The energy radiating from Mal always left tremors upon the air. And a kind of light that made things brighter, like river-sheen, or that moment held at the peak of ecstasy when all shadows vanish.

Mal's hard cock pressed against the back of Dare's thigh. He loved to feel that, knowing he was wanted. But right now he could not bring himself to turn and curve himself into that pleasure.

The candles guttered. Moonlight streamed through the un-curtained double doors at the balcony, along with a cool breeze.

Dare's eyes were wide open. A goblet on the wooden table glimmered faintly in the dim light. He watched it as if hypnotized. He didn't want to think. He couldn't *not* think.

Everything he'd done up to now had been at Prince Darius's behest. It had all led to the best of dreams and the worst of nightmares. But grandest of all, it had led him to Mal.

Now the tight knot of souls they had woven together through their love was threatened. He could feel it all around him. Around *them.* A peril to their very beings because of Brookfall's king and his paranoid delusions, his desire for war.

He could not help but flash back on his short time in the dungeon, with Stix in his fine clothes, proper and tall, clear-eyed and conscienceless. He remembered the words Stix had told him. Everyone wore masks. Everyone had something to hide. Stix could not know how dangerously true his words were, for Stix and the others still had no clue he wasn't a true prince.

The scars on Dare's back itched at the memory. Of guilt. Of a beating he actually may have deserved. Of anguish because, no, he really didn't deserve any of this madness. The muscles beneath his scars shivered.

"You're shaking," Mal said, wrapping his arms tighter about Dare's waist.

"I'm cold."

"Bu the night is warm. I can grab more covers."

"No. I'm cold inside."

Mal's lips pressed gently against his bare shoulder. Dare took that tenderness inside him, trying to light his way with it. Flailing. His eyes stung. He closed them tight. Held his breath.

They'd been over and over options, none of them viable. Mal could not tell his father the truth. It was treason. They both worried King Millard would not protect them. Millard was not a bad king, but he and Mal had a testy relationship at best.

The queen had already shown her distaste for Dare even as she pretended to accept him into the royal family. She would be no help.

Running away was an idea, but Dare wanted it to be a last resort. The guilt of taking Mal away from his kingdom and family would eat at him until his last days. Dare wanted to be sure Mal had everything he deserved. This option to run guaranteed a lifetime of regret and resentments between them. It remained in the back of his mind that, yes, they could run, but only after they had tried everything.

Dare opened his eyes again. The shadows of the room blurred. Mal's lips on his shoulder had moved. He pressed his cheek there now, and slowly ran his fingers through Dare's hair. The hardness against the back of Dare's thigh had receded a bit.

He could feel the tension in Mal, now. The prince was just as worried, but he showed it differently. And he wasn't the liar that Dare was. He wasn't the pretender. He only loved the pretender. Dare's crime was far greater. He had to answer for it if only deep inside himself.

He would be getting no sleep tonight.

*

Days passed in a hazy sort of emotional paralysis for Dare. They were scheduled to leave for the border soon. But soon would not come fast enough.

No longer did the two young men rush about the gardens making love wherever they could find a hide-away. No longer did their eyes meet in glowing reverence over meals or meetings or games of backgammon. They spent all their time together, but they did not talk as much as they used to. They did not make love at all.

Dare's body ached at the loss. It physically hurt. The fever of love had been replaced by a fever of impending doom.

Mal became shorter-tempered with the guards, his grooms, even the king and queen.

The morning before they were to disembark on their journey to the border, Mal became particularly nasty to his guards when they'd knocked for entrance and, not receiving a quick enough reply, opened the doors. As they always had.

"I don't care if the fucking king himself commands you, you are not to barge into my rooms without warning. Ever. Not for the king's command, not for any reason.

The guard in question stood firm, but the tension in his shoulders and arms, and the way he bunched his fists, told Dare that he was very close to breaking, or murdering Prince Malory himself.

44

"Now fucking get out!" Mal yelled.

The guard hesitated before turning.

"I will have your head for that!" Mal burst out, then slammed his fist against the ornate, wood door. It banged shut in the guard's face.

Dare stood in the center of their room, once the prince's chamber but now theirs, a marriage chamber, a place where they were supposed to live and love and find their peace tangled together in mutual ardor and adulation.

The way the light touched Mal, Dare thought he might be seeing actual steam rising from him. The fumes of anger made the room seem sharp and unwelcoming in that moment.

Dare still toyed with their last resort plan. They could leave. That might be the best and only answer. But they had time. They could still make that decision, even on the road.

Mal gave out a strange roar. He made a fist and hit the wall beside the door, then yowled at the pain.

Dare rushed to him, coming up from behind and putting his arms around him. It was like holding a wild thing, like holding fear and rage and animosity all trapped inside the beautiful man he loved. But instead of struggling, Mal turned into Dare's embrace, facing him, hands on his shoulders.

Dare bent his head and pressed his forehead into Mal's chest.

"I'm sorry. This is all my doing, this hurt, this pain. I shouldn't have continued my disguise. I should never—"

"Don't!" Mal's fingers tightened on Dare's shoulders. He pushed him back with a stormy force. He shook Dare. Once. Twice. Three times.

Dare looked up at him. "My crime. It's my crime. I should just confess—"

"Shut up. Shut up!" He shook Dare hard again. "Shut up!" Then he shoved him away.

Dare stumbled back. So far Mal had never taken his anger out on him. But the stress of tomorrow was too much.

They'd be leaving. And their actions would either stop or cause a war. One or both of them might not survive.

It was all too much.

Mal's honey-colored eyes were crazy, the pupils wide and black. Normally, they were beautiful, adoring whenever Mal looked at Dare. Now they glittered with an iciness that was almost ugly, as if every good thing about Mal had been taken, as if they held nothing more than the stare of a man who had already lost the battle he cared most about.

"Don't speak," came Mal's devastated voice. "I cannot stand to hear—"

"My voice?"

Mal was silent. They stared at each other. Dare's chest trembled. He could not manage a deep breath.

Mal's lips curved downward in a scowl.

And Dare thought, *This is it. We can't live through this. Even our love, like molten gold, cannot survive this.*

Then as suddenly as Mal's outrage came on, it crumpled. His eyes softened and filled. With a rough edge to his voice, he said, "I didn't mean that."

Dare stepped closer to him. His own tears blurred his vision but did not spill. He started to take another step, but Mal leapt forward and grabbed him, hugging him tight, leaning back and nearly picking Dare up off the floor. Their foreheads knocked together. Their faces met. Their lips.

Dare's mouth opened and Mal's tongue was there, locking them together in a kiss so torrid and tight that Dare was instantly hard and almost coming from the intensity. It had been too long since they'd fucked, made love, or just kissed.

Their bodies knew it. Voracious, they were nearly exploding against each other. The stress, the terror of their situation, all of it consumed them but their bodies still needed each other. Longing. Desire. The ache could not be ignored or appeased, to be inside each other, holding, caressing, careening together toward unknowns made of the breath of silver stars, created from the bliss of ancient passions that the soul rules and cannot thrive without.

They were one another's air and water and fuel and heart. Without each other, only weakness, fear and fury remained. Only dissipation.

The kiss and the hot embrace sent Dare into a realm of white sky. There was no ground, no *grounding* except Mal's body surrounding him, creating catastrophes within him of passion and lust. Sensuality. And such drastic and drenching love that he would crush kingdoms to keep it. In this moment, he would madly lash out at anyone who tried to stop this love.

He wanted to weep and shout and stab and scream.

Mal grunted against his mouth, not letting up even for a breath. He nearly picked Dare up, dragging him to the bed.

Hands were everywhere before Dare fell back on the covers, pulling at shirts and belts and boots. Their mouths lost each other for a moment that felt like panic and death and the life of breath all at once.

Mal's wild hair tickled Dare's chest, shirtless now, as he strained to remove his boots and Dare's. Once that task was done, their trousers followed, tossed aside like banners on the wind.

Dare's cock was so hard it stretched tight against his belly, already wet at the tip.

Mal's cock slid thick and heavy against the front of Dare's thigh as he bent and scooped Dare's cock into his mouth, sucking all the way down.

Dare's body went rigid with the shock of such pleasure, and he reached out blindly and raked his fingers hard across Mal's shoulders, pulling him down harder until Mal choked.

Dare had never been so inconsiderate, but he was a madman now. Nothing mattered but Mal and their passion. They were starved. Pathetically sick. For each other. Nothing else was real.

Dare felt his balls twitch, and the passion built, but Mal pulled away before it crested, pushing him up in the bed, hands on the backs of his thighs, bending his legs up until Dare's ass came up, bare and open for his lover to see.

Mal spit on his fingers and rammed two up his hole before Dare could even blink.

All right, this was not going to be tender. This was not going to be gentle.

And that was fine.

He wanted all the pent up passion and love with the rage, with the resentments. He wanted to be taken and pushed and fucked and loved until he could not see, until he was a mess of bone and flesh. He wanted everything Mal had to give hard and fast and furious.

The entire universe, he was convinced, was holding its breath for this.

Dare sat up fast, grabbing Mal about the waist, pulling him up and up.

"Wha—" Mal fell back a little as Dare's bent, head coming forward, mouth grazing Mal's cock.

Mal fell back on his ass, legs stretching forward, spreading.

"If you're going to do it like that, you have to be wet," Dare commanded, before taking Mal's cock in his mouth and sliding it down his throat.

Mal moaned.

Dare knew he was close so he tried not to suck, but only slick him with his spit.

Satisfied when he felt Mal's cock glide as if on oil from his mouth, he fell back, legs in the air and said, "Do it."

Mal gave a yell of triumph and positioned himself.

"Don't take your time!" Dare spoke through gritted teeth.

Mal pushed in and Dare screamed. It felt raw. It hurt. It was so good.

In seconds his body accepted the intruder and Mal began to thrust. The tip of his cock slid against Dare's sweet spot making his vision spark.

Dare yelled out as bliss, such a sweet and pretty word, threatened to slice him into a million pieces and toss him about the room.

As Mal thrust toward his own pleasure, Dare's stiff cock thumped against his stomach over and over. He reached between their bodies, grabbing it, milking from base to tip again and again.

He'd never been so ready to burst into flame. So high. So broken and whole at the same time. So ready. So ready.

Let go, said a voice inside him. *Let go! Let me go!*

He was taking off now, a swan in the whiteness, white on white, sleek and shining, wet from the lake and the rain and the tears.

Now the sky became an embrace. He floated, broke apart.

Dimly, as if awareness existed down a lane far from the center of life, he felt hot dampness spray his stomach and chest. It lasted for a long long time, and the man inside him moved and churned him even more, so the rain came white and hot. On him. Within him. And two male cries mingled in the morning light.

Even the king and queen had to have heard it. This time. The crashing of their hearts.

Chapter Seven

The afterglow came upon them, unlike their lovemaking, with a gentle and tender hand. Mal fell across Dare's body, damp, still hard, and trembling. Dare lifted his arms around him, stroking his smooth, lean back. They were both still trying to catch their breaths.

Slowly, Dare raised one arm and pushed his fingers through Mal's untamed curls. Like brambles, they were, only softer.

Mal lifted his head until they could look into each other's eyes. Dare saw devotion. And awe. No more hard edges. Mal's passion remained but the temper from earlier was, for now, relieved.

They kissed delicately, a meeting of lips, drawn out, a slow rubbing and sweet licks that went no further than the openings of their mouths. Even so, the affection in the gesture made Dare dizzy.

Eventually, Mal rolled off Dare and they lay face to face on their sides, naked on top of the bedcovers, running their hands up and down each other's shoulders, flanks, chests.

They stared into each other's eyes for more long moments, then kissed again.

When they broke off for breath, Mal said, "You're everything."

Dare's throat closed with emotion. Mal sounded both lost and wonderstruck at the same time.

When Dare did not respond, Mal said, "I never want you apart from my side."

Dare finally found his voice. "I don't, either."

Mal reached between them and picked up Dare's hand in his, interlocking their fingers. "We will do whatever we need to do. We will not be apart."

Dare nodded, silent. He squeezed Mal's palm.

"We cannot be afraid," Mal said.

"But I am."

"I love you." Mal's other hand came up to cup Dare's cheek. "We love each other. This will always be."

Dare swallowed dryly. "Always?"

"Yes. In life, no matter what. And in death and after. Always."

When Dare breathed in, his lungs shivered. He didn't like Mal talking about death. There had been too much death in Dare's past already. But he said nothing.

Mal leaned forward and kissed him until the shivering stopped.

*

The horses were brought round by the stable boys, and they whinnied through the early morning fog.

Dare had not been able to eat a bite at breakfast. As he mounted Midnight, his stomach was a knot.

Today was the big day. King Millard had agreed to their amended plan to a meeting at the border. He had actually listened when Mal had argued that Dare's safety—his husband's safety--was in question if they went all the way into Brookfall. He had actually agreed with Mal that this meet and greet was the best way for the foreigner king to see that his son was unharmed. They would return the ransom at the meeting. Dare would then return to Shastan.

In reality, Dare and Mal would work to convince the king of Brookfall that Dare still impersonated a *living* Prince Darius, and all was well. If they had to, they would beg for peace. They would appeal to the king of Brookfall's charity and love for his broken son who, feeling abandoned, was unwilling to see him.

Thus, they were going to the border, a day and a half ride, to see the king of Brookfall.

A dozen royal guards, three grooms for the horses, and half a dozen other servants were to accompany them. They would meet up half-way with a regiment of the king's army comprised of a thousand well-trained soldiers.

This was no small move on King Millard's part. He took the threat of war seriously, as well as the safety of his son and son-in-law. He planned for the contingency that the returned ransom might be taken as an affront. He wanted his son and son-in-law protected.

Yet Dare had never felt more vulnerable, wrong, and out of place.

Mal came up alongside him, his horse dancing side to side, ready to go.

"Everything will be all right."

Dare glanced away. He knew Mal was not trying to lie to him, but they were just words to placate him. It wasn't working.

Mal said, "I have an addition to our plan. I didn't discuss it with you because it's still being set up. You must trust me."

Dare turned to stare at him, not willing to allow himself even the tiniest surge of hope. "Why didn't you tell me?"

"Because I just thought of it this morning when I was in the stables overseeing the picks for the extra horses." He gave Dare a quick grin. "Trust me."

He did trust Mal. It was the plan—any plan—he questioned. Despite their renewed and urgent lovemaking, the restlessness of doom would not leave Dare.

He could not question Mal more for at that moment the group began to move out of the courtyard, over the castle grounds and the pathway that lead by the large pond and to the gates.

Everything was dew-damp, still, and the fog, though thinning, made it difficult to see beyond the green edges of the bushes, and the willows that lined the pond. The towers above the gates looked shrouded in dissipating clouds. Summer days were warm, but in the deepest hours before morning, a cool dampness etched itself into the air, and then began the rolling mists.

Dare wore his favorite green cloak, a gift from Mal when he was in the dungeon and at one of his lowest points. Within an hour of riding it would no doubt be discarded, carefully rolled and packed into his saddlebag.

Strung taut, Dare's nerves jumped. His dark and dreary thoughts swam. *Will this be the last summer I ever see?* And, *I cannot bear it if Mal is ever hurt by what I've done.*

Mal rode ahead, a Shastan prince clad in a golden cloak the same color as his unruly hair. He rode with an unconscious majesty, the privilege he was born to. Dare had doubled for Prince Darius enough times that he knew how to comport himself in regal fashion. His education had been even better than Darius's since he'd done most of Darius's homework for him, but it was still always a thought on his mind, his deception, not natural-born to him to actually *be* a prince.

What thoughts must be in Mal's mind at this moment? Mal had a plan. Mal always had a plan these past two weeks. That didn't mean it was a good one. Dare wanted to know, and yet he didn't. It would just be another outlandish brainstorm to add to their dilemma of how to keep Dare's secret that he was impersonating a *dead* prince once they met the Brookfall king.

Dare concentrated on the clomping footfalls of the horses, the squeaky wheels of the supply carriage, and the birds calling back and forth through the misty fields. The fragrant scents of narcissus and trumpet vines powdered the air. Gone were the poppies, which carpeted the fields for only a few weeks in spring.

They passed groves of wild oak and olive. The fog receded rapidly. Soon Dare was sweating, and he put his cloak away.

When they stopped for lunch, Dare brushed dried moss from a fallen log and sat, watching as the grooms saw to Midnight. Mal came toward him, his lips pressed tight. Dare had not seen him smile in a long time.

Dare glanced nervously to Mal's left, not meeting his eyes.

"What's this new plan? It can't be better than simply facing the king and telling him Darius sent me in his stead and hope no one else in our party hears the lie but you and me." Dare spoke low, almost in a whisper. The servants and guard ignored them.

"Another imposter," Mal said, as if the solution were that simple.

A wind rustled through the tops of the nearby trees. It ruffled Mal's hair.

Dare blinked. "Wh-what?"

"I found him in the stables this morning and had my epiphany. He's a rough boy, but looks enough like you. I hired him on." Mal raised his hand over his eyes, scanning through the crowd of horses, past the supply wagon, and the guards that surrounded them, ever vigilant, still on duty. "He's over there. One of the grooms. See?"

Dare squinted in the direction Mal indicated. A boy took two horses into a clearing to graze. He had dark hair falling across his brow, and was the same height as Dare. But they did not look alike. The boy's chin was too pointed, his nose crooked as if once broken by a rearing horse.

"It should have been the first thing we came up with," Mal continued, voice low and soft. "Your Prince Darius always had a double. Right?"

Dare nodded, still watching the boy as he stroked the sleek neck of the horse nearest him.

"Why wouldn't Darius continue that game? He hates the public eye. He even hates his father now, for what he's done? Why wouldn't he send a double to meet him and not come face to face himself?"

"But the king isn't that stupid," Dare said. "He won't go for a proxy that isn't me. And maybe not even for me."

"But it goes to credibility. Darius used you as a double all the time. It makes sense that if he was alive, he'd continue to use proxies."

"The king will still demand to see him."

Mal swallowed, nodding slowly.

"He'll wipe the floor with that boy," Dare continued. "The boy won't even know what to do, to say, how to answer anything. And we have a day to train him. It won't work."

"Then what do you suggest?" Mal asked. "It's the best I've got right now. Are you simply going to walk in and tell the truth? Because I can't let you do that. I'll abduct you myself and take you to far-off Creaopolis before that happens."

Creaopolis was a fairytale. A word they used to describe some unseen, distant paradise. Their own private code for escape. They'd talked about the distant countries they might sneak off to. Middle-of-nowhere, barbaric realms, ideal places for hiding but not for much else than avoiding crime, local skirmishes, and abduction into slavery in countries where it was still legal.

They would have money. Prince Malory had treasure enough to see them through as long as highwaymen didn't steal it all out from under them during their voyages. It was entirely laughable. All paths were theoretical at the moment, and highly idealistic. Any calamity could befall them on the road. It was already hard enough for Dare to pretend he was a prince. But to pretend he was a prince pretending he wasn't a prince was also laughable. Of course he could do it. He knew how to be the best of servants, honorable and loyal. But Mal? Mal would not be able to pull it off. How could he stop holding himself so high in the saddle? And how could Mal successfully hide his bearing, his demeanor, that arrogant gaze that expected others to obey him before he uttered one word? A man who did that didn't even know he was doing it.

One might fake being a prince. But to fake *not* being a prince after being born to it would be the most difficult of tasks. Especially if guards were sent after them, and people in villages and townships were on the lookout for the runaway prince with the glowing curls of golden hair.

Mal was smart, but he would eventually misstep. Dare's mind ran a hundred scenarios where that might happen. And then it would be over for them both. Forever. Mal would be returned to a kingdom that might spare him but never accept him as their king, and Dare would be headed straight for the chopping block.

Dare kept silent. But his heart would not stop jerking in his chest. He had nothing to say about Creaopolis, or their new plan. In his deepest heart, he would never run. To run would guarantee war. Thousands would die and it would be his fault. He could not live with himself if that were the case. Mal still talked about that plan, and Dare let him because Mal had to have options. Even that one. But Dare would never run.

He rummaged for his water flask. He sipped the water, and thought of better times.

Mal seemed lost in thought.

The cook brought them plates of bread, cheese and thinly sliced, dried beef. They made sandwiches out of it. Everything tasted like ash to Dare. Even with no breakfast, and a long ride, he felt little hunger.

He remembered his last travels through these lands, how sick he'd been.

He forced himself to eat.

*

They'd made good time in one long day. The Great Forest was thinning.

Dare was so tired, he was seeing faces in the trees and in the meadow grasses of the flowering glens they passed.

56

When he dismounted, a tremble of light-headedness made the world spin. Midnight stood very still, chomping the bit, as Dare leaned against the horse's neck to gather his wits. The animal's sweat was pungent but comforting. A known fact. The scent brought him round.

Mal's hand on his shoulder completed a circle with the horse and the ground that gave him balance. In that moment, Dare loved Mal more than ever. His heart fluttered.

One more night. One more day. That was all they had before the meet.

The servants had the royal tent pitched quickly, the bedding and chests brought in, everything neatly arranged.

Dare nearly collapsed on the bed. When he opened his eyes, Mal had two bowls of stew in his hands, still steaming. He placed them on the table inside the tent.

Dare got up and joined him for the meal. It was spiced just how he liked it and he ate every bit.

Unlike last time when he'd come through the Great Forest, this was not some physical ailment that made him feel sick. It was emotional this time, and though his body did not ache, the torment seemed far, far worse than any fever.

The ale was strong tonight. Mal refilled Dare's goblet twice.

"Drink up," Mal said. "You need to sleep well tonight."

Dare did as he was told.

He barely remembered dragging himself to bed and Mal's arms coming around him, the cushion and blankets cocooning them both. The sounds of the men outside the canvas panels of the tent faded. The night purred with crickets.

Twice Dare jerked awake, his heart leaping frantically beneath his ribs. With Mal's warmth beside him, he settled in and slept some more.

Chapter Eight

They approached King Millard's regiment before noon the following day. The border was less than an hour away now. Banners flew along the front line of the soldiers horses, the pennants emblazoned with the unicorn silhouette, the crest of Shastan.

Surrounded by so many men who'd made vows to the king to protect them, Dare should have felt safer.

He did not.

Often, he stared at the groomsman who resembled himself and Prince Darius in all but the refined structures of the face. He watched the way the boy whispered to the horses and how their ears flickered to hear his words, how he cared for them, and rode with ease speaking in soft undertones that soothed.

The boy had a calmness about him, and a decent bearing, but the king of Brookfall was no horse, and Dare could not imagine sending the young man in to face an angry king in a matter of such grave concern as the possibility of war between two nations who had been enemies for so long.

No. The boy should not have to go into that royal tent as proxy for Prince Darius.

Dare would have to go himself. As they'd already planned beforehand. Dare would have to figure out how to convince the king that his son was alive and more paranoid than ever, and refused to come into the Brookfall camp. The king of Brookfall would just have to accept he would not be able to see his son.

Would it work? Of course not. But they had to try. It was the only sane option.

*

They rode a thousand strong.

The Great Forest gave way to more and more clearings, and then the early summer fields of wild barley, clover and dandelions appeared. The tree-line vanished, and Dare could see the distant mountain range of Brookfall where the castle keep stood over-looking a green valley, a river, and wondrous hundred-foot waterfalls. He could not see the castle, of course, they were still a long day's journey away from there, but the bluish-purple range gave him a start, and he felt a lump in his throat.

Though his child ghost wandered there, he hoped never to go back.

As the first line of horses and riders stepped into the broadest meadow, butterflies and dragonflies flitted up like pieces of gilt etching their language into the air.

The beauty blurred, however, when Dare saw in the far distance a glimmer of silver and dark knots of movement on the horizon. Behind that, dots of white and dirty gray littered the landscape. Pavilions. Cook-tents. Lean-tos and sleeping structures. Tiny fumes of smoke curled into the air.

They had arrived at the border. Brookfall encampment was minutes away.

Mal murmured under his breath, as if talking to his horse, "Easy. Easy."

Dare glanced at him, but Mal kept his gaze straight ahead.

The sounds around them of horses snorting, men's murmurs rising in the air, and the ringing of insects in the wild grasses mixed with the butterflies on the drowsy air gave the scene a dreamy quality. Or, more, a nightmare as they headed toward Dare's people, toward the enemy.

When they were close enough to see the blackbird crest on the banners of the Brookfall encampment, they stopped. They were not quite within shouting distance, so a mediator was sent as ambassador to meet with a mediator from Brookfall for the final set up of the meeting.

Dare and Mal were surrounded by guards at all times as they slid off their horses. Servants rushed about, preparing to build a makeshift camp, seeing to royal needs first.

Mal shouted orders here and there. Dare remained silent. Someone thrust a goblet of wine into his hands. He almost dropped it. As he stared at the liquid sloshing against the sides of metal cup, he realized his hands were shaking.

Mal jogged up to him, grass crunching under his booted footfalls.

"Drink it," he said. "It will help."

"You keep ordering me to get drunk. How will that help?"

"It will help you," Mal replied.

Dare shook his head.

"You aren't calm, and you need to be if this is going to work." Mal glanced over his shoulder to make sure no one was too near them to overhear his words. "I've met with the groom. His name is Verick. He is loyal to me and therefore to you. He has agreed to impersonate you before the king, telling him it is by order of Prince Darius. He did not ask questions. He is a servant and that means he lives to serve and look the other way."

"I know what it means to be a servant." Dare's whisper came out a bit harsh.

Mal took a breath as if ready to respond, then closed his mouth.

Dare said, "He won't be able to answer questions. He won't stand a chance in front of the shrewdness of the king."

"I will be at his side at all times. I will make sure your king gets his answers."

Your king. Dare's king. Darius's father. Everything he was doing now was beyond any mere definition of treason.

Mal reached out and touched his arm. "Dare. You are saving lives. This is stopping a war. Keep that forefront in your mind."

"I'm not going to have Verick go in my place. I'm going."

Dare glanced about, looking for a place to set down his wine so it wouldn't spill. Already, their tent had been erected, the last of the stakes being pounded into place. A table was set up just outside the front flaps. Dare went to it and set down the goblet.

Mal followed alongside. "That's not what we discussed, what we agreed to."

The chiming of the insects had quieted a bit. The afternoon was placid, with a slight breeze that made the dandelions bob as if falling off to sleep. Their seeds wafted upon the air like snow out of season.

"I know. But I need to see the king. To explain why Darius won't see him. I've known him my whole life. He hasn't been a father to me, not really, but he has shown me respect. He'll believe me. He won't believe anyone but me. I'm the only one who can do this."

A strange look came over Mal's face, both sad and angry and helpless all at the same time. Dare did not like seeing that look, but there was no other way.

"I won't risk you," Mal hissed. Then, his voice broke. "I won't."

"You have no choice."

A servant came up, arms loaded with bedding. He tried to enter the tent.

Mal whirled on him. "Leave us for a few moments." He grabbed Dare and steered him into the empty tent for privacy.

"There are choices!" Mal said.

"Not this time," Dare said firmly.

"We'll run, then."

"No! I can't live if I know I'm responsible for a war. The king's guard would come after us and find us anyway."

"Well, if your plan works, you'll be king one day. You'll be responsible for life and death and war if it comes to it." Mal said this almost as a threat.

Dare could not even think that far ahead. King? Mal would be king. Yes. But Dare?

A feeling of pain gripped his stomach.

Dare turned away from Mal and stared at the blank, heavy canvas of the tent. His throat threatened to close but his eyes were clear.

"If it comes to that, life, death, war, I will make my choices then, just as I am now. I wasn't born to this. But what does it make me into if I have a boy face a king for me?"

He thought about Prince Darius making him face the public, courtiers, ambassadors, royalty. Darius had already given up on everything he'd been born to while still a child. And he had died for it. His choice had killed him. He'd been afraid of everything yet hadn't seemed to care about dying. Dying had been a reprieve for Darius. A way to hide himself away with finality.

Dare was the opposite of his master. Always had been. He did not face the world through fear. He could not imagine living that way. He'd lived too long locked up, first in Darius's rooms obeying every whim of the prince. They hardly ever left the castle. And later, locked in a room at Shastan decorated in neckbands and chains.

Closing his eyes and fists, Dare said, "We cannot be ruled by fear."

"But we all are," said Mal from behind.

Dare heard clothing rustle, felt the warmth of his lover come up behind him.

"All the time," Mal added.

"And I am afraid," Dare replied. "But I will face him, not Verick. It's my duty. It's the right thing to do."

Mal opened his mouth. Closed it. Obviously moved. After a long moment, he took a deep breath. "What will you say?"

Dare felt Mal touch his waist, a light caress, palm warm against his clothing and the skin beneath.

"I have a million thoughts in my head. All at once. I can't quiet them. I can't know until I see him. I can't plan this one ahead…"

"You will *not* tell him the truth." Mal said it as a command.

Slowly, Dare turned. His eyes were hot as they met Mal's gaze. "I have been excellent at lying so far." His voice felt unsteady.

Mal's brows narrowed. "You've done it to save lives."

Dare nodded. "Yes. And my own life."

"Men cannot be faulted for that."

"Men *are* faulted for that. It's why we still keep this secret."

Mal glanced away as if annoyed. "It's gone beyond your life, or mine. That's why."

Dare softened his voice. "I know. But it's going too far. Essentially, I am asking the king of Brookfall to accept *me* as his heir."

"Dare." Mal lifted his hands and put them on Dare's shoulders. He looked at Dare again, all irritation gone, the corners of his mouth and eyes relaxed. "You are not a bad person. You aren't scheming and your agendas are for the well-being of others. You were helping Prince Darius. You got caught I his and his father's web. You can't help it if one day the route you take to cause less harm accidentally makes you a king. A king is a piece on a chessboard. Right now you stand outside the chessboard dressed as a prince. If the pieces look to you for the next move, it's not your fault. It's fate."

"Fate," Dare repeated.

"Yes. And there's not a damn thing you can do about it."

"But I never wanted to be a king."

"I was born to it. I had no choice, either," Mal countered.

"That's different."

"How? This is the road you're on now. How you got here makes no difference. You need to make the best of it to save our two kingdoms."

"I know I need to make the best choices I can," Dare replied. "When I face the king, I'll make him believe that Prince Darius is still alive."

"And I will be there at your side. I will help you." He bowed his head in rare deference.

Dare nodded. Mal's hands on his shouldered grounded him. Dare did not touch him in return. Instead, he put a hand to his head and leaned for a moment into his own strength.

"I think this is what we should do," Dare said. "I'll want Verick dressed in a prince's attire. Cloak his head. Have the guards stand with him at the edge of the meadow."

"What will you do?" Mal asked.

"I don't know. I don't know yet, but I need him there. As if he is Darius. As if Darius is here but keeping his distance."

"Brilliant. I see what you're thinking. It will be done," Mal said. He leaned in, placing a soft kiss to Dare's forehead.

Despite the stress and weariness, and the churning feeling that this might be his last day on Earth, Dare's skin flushed at the gesture. His body grew instantly warm. Mal was everything he wanted. All the room in his heart had been given to Mal. It was the most euphoric sensation to know this without a doubt, and in this moment he had no regrets for the unfortunate journey that had brought them together.

*

When the mediator returned, they learned the meeting was set for two hours before sunset.

That did not give them long to bathe and change into fancier garb fit to meet a king. And to have Verick instructed as to his part in the deception.

When they met Verick in the servant's tent, he was already dressed in white and black with a velvet waistcoat in gold that matched Dare's. Dare recognized a beloved servant of Mal's trimming Verick's long dark hair in the style Dare wore, combed back and to the side, his locks brushing his shoulders.

The scissor nearly took his eye out as Verick went to his knees and bowed before the intruding princes.

"Your Highnesses!"

Every servant in the tent knelt before them.

Mal said, "Stand. All of you. As you were."

He beckoned Verick closer. Verick came forward, head down. He wore a prince's clothing, but his shoulders slumped, his hair still fell into his eyes and he kept moving his head back and forth in a nervous manner.

Dare thought: *He doesn't look like Darius at all. Or me.*

Darius may have been secluded by his own choice, and unfriendly, but not in this way. Not shy. Not scared of people one on one. With people, Darius had been spiteful and bullying, laughing at their expense, looking to make them feel even less than they were. He loved that sort of power over others, just not in the ways princehood or kingship demanded. He would never have bowed his head or bend his back and shoulders downward. He would never dart his gaze about as if he didn't know where to look.

And the worst? He probably would have met his father one on one in this circumstance.

Dare was going to have to be quick and smart about his explanations.

In the meantime, he said to Verick, "Ease up. When you're in these clothes you must not look down, or bow. Look up at me, please."

Mal stood back and watched.

Verick's eyes were green like the meadows. Not brown. It wouldn't be a problem if no one from Brookfall saw those eyes. Or that face.

"Stand tall."

Verick obeyed. Unsure. And obviously nervous to have the attention of two princes directly upon him.

"You will be seen from a distance by the men of Brookfall. All you must do is look the part of a prince. You do not have to speak to anyone. Do you understand?"

"Yes, Your Highness." He shifted from foot to foot.

Mal stepped forward. "Verick," he said softly.

Verick looked up at him with open adoration, skin flushing.

"You understand," Mal continued, "that you are to do this without question. I know it seems strange but we, Prince Darius and I, have our reasons. The guards I have chosen will guard you well. You do not have to know why you will be standing at a distance doubling for Prince Darius. But understand it is for the safety of all of us. And I will guarantee your safety."

"Yes, Your Highness." By the tone in Verick's voice, he would lay down his life for the prince. Without question. But for Dare? Verick mostly offered him nervous glances, nothing more.

When it came to the guards, Dare thought they might have problems with the strangeness of Mal's requests. But all Mal said to them was, "Make sure Verick is within sight of the king's tent. Cloaked. Hood up but folded back enough to show his black hair and the cut of it. Make sure he stands in profile, please."

He did not say anything about why Verick was wearing a prince's clothing. Or he why he wanted Verick to be *seen*.

Dare expected questions, or at least wary looks on the faces of the guards.

But the guards merely bowed, startling the air with their clear voices.

"Yes, Your Highness!"

"Yes, my Lord!"

All were nervous. They knew the prince's life could be in danger. The meeting was a crucial landmark toward peace. That was the truth Dare was playing out.

Technically, King Millard should have been in attendance for such an auspicious scene. The king of Brookfall would take insult to that absence, no doubt, as well as everything around him.

But if King Millard had come, Dare knew everything would have been even more complicated. The king would question what Mal and Dare were doing. Worse, he would attend the meeting and not understand why the father of Prince Darius did not recognize his own son.

They had been lucky that King Millard had entrusted this huge move on the chessboard of reality to his son. The king of Shastan rarely traveled anymore, and Dare did not question his decision.

But leaving King Millard behind was a slight to Brookfall.

Mal told Dare that the most important meeting of the kings would be at the actual signing of a peace treaty. Because there was no guarantee that would ever occur, the king was safer back at the palace, allowing his son to command the troops and negotiate. That had been Mal's explanation for King Millard's decision not to accompany them. But Dare had wondered if King Millard had other thoughts about the matter, or even suspected that Dare kept secrets.

It seemed every move they made led to more twists and turns and dead-ends.

The story of their strange behavior with Verick would eventually get back to the king. Rumors flew fast and wide in all royal courts. When they returned they would have many things to answer for. If they survived.

This was a maze started with the real Prince Darius's death, and it would never end until Dare himself stopped breathing.

Chapter Nine

Despite the murmurs of tense men, the shifts of armor, and vast line ups of ready soldiers sitting on impatient mounts in the distance all around them, the day was idyllic. Wood thrushes and chickadees sang in the fields. Above, the sky was an eye-searing blue. The small herds of back-up horses whinnied in a friendly manner as they grazed peacefully on either side of the border.

The wind held a sweetness one could not help but savor. The insects happily feasted on budding pollens. The golden sunlight left its molten sheen upon Mal's hair.

Dare was ready to move to move forward and see the king.

Though he appreciated Mal at his side adding a force of energy and hope, he was at the cusp of things inside his own mind. At times like these, all thought of hope or dread vanished and he was inside the moment. A moment where sky and rock, enemy and lover were images undirected by him, out of his control. All he could do was control his own next steps, his own propulsion through this moment and into the next.

Two contingents of guards on foot surrounded Dare and Mal, those wearing the blackbird emblem, and those wearing the unicorn. All were armed.

Mal and Dare had been instructed to leave behind their swords. To meet the king of Brookfall alone and in private, the rule came loud and clear. No swords. No knives. Nothing that could be construed as a weapon. The guards kept theirs, but they would not be going inside the tent.

Dare spared a glance across the meadow toward the semi-circle of guards who stood close to a solitary figure in a dark red cloak. His heart jumped. Verick looked so small, and was not standing tall like a prince at all. Also, he seemed too far away.

Dare elbowed Mal, saying softly, "Verick needs to be closer."

Mal followed Dare's gaze. "He's fine."

"You can't see him clearly enough. I mean his figure, his posture. And it's all wrong anyway, the way he's standing." His voice came out low, almost cracking through his tense throat.

Mal gave a quick order to one of the guards closest to him. Dare turned away, but noted the guard left, heading toward Verick in the distance.

*

The king's pavilion had gold-bordered dags, each stamped with an impression of a blackbird in flight. Dare had seen it before. It was not a battlefield tent. The king of Brookfall used it for outdoor events on the castle grounds including summer hunts, autumn dances, and spring fairs when citizens from nearby townships and farms came to feast and celebrate the season.

It gave Dare the feeling that the king intended this meet to be a peaceful one.

Three gold balls topped the pavilion at its apex; below hung a skirt of red which curved gently to drape the white canvas roof. The sides were striped red and black and looked slightly weather-worn but strong enough to hold the wind back, and even winter rain and sleet. A canvas awning, also red, stretched out from the entrance. Hemp ropes were staked to either side, keeping it taut, unmoving.

It was a decent sized structure, big enough to house a throne along with three feasting tables each seating eight. Dare had been inside the tent during festivals. And feasts.

Beneath the awning, a trail of carpet had been laid out. Also red. The drapes to the entrance had been tied back. Two armored and armed guards stood to either side of the drapes, attention-stiff. Both had tall staffs and heavy broadswords at their belts.

Dare could no longer hear a thing, not the insects, not the murmurs of the men, not even his own footsteps or breath. He was aware of Mal at his side, but he felt as if he was far far away.

One of the guards said, "The king bids you enter alone, Your Highness." The voice of the guard sounded small and soft, as if spoken through gauze.

"Is *he* alone?" Dare asked, glancing rapidly at Mal.

No breath. Nothing but a feeling of timelessness as he waited for the guard to answer.

"He has an advisor with him. Lord Brandon."

Luckily, Dare did not know Lord Brandon. But had Prince Darius known him? The king had many advisors and they changed over the years at the king's whim. Darius ignored them all since he'd never been invited to a council session. Still, any advisor might know him on sight.

Mal stiffened beside him. He leaned close to Dare, his breath on his ear. "Is this a problem?"

"Aside from the king knowing immediately who I am?" Dare asked.

Mal went silent.

"My own advisor is the prince of Shastan. He will be allowed entry at my side or I will leave." Dare held his head up, his shoulders tightly back.

"It is you and you alone the king will see," the guard replied.

At his side, Dare felt Mal's hand brush against his own. Mal was unarmed but their own guard stood only a step away.

"My husband will accompany me," Dare said. "The King of Brookfall's son-in-law. Would you deprive the king from meeting one of his own family?"

The guard now looked confused as he glanced from Dare to Mal and back to Dare again.

"This was the agreement. That I accompany Prince Darius. You dare to question it?" Mal asked bluntly. He wore a circlet of thin bronze in his curls. He looked and sounded like a royal heir and future king. His charisma was natural; his power could not be ignored.

The guard finally nodded with one hard jerk of his head.

Mal and Dare stepped under the awning.

Dare saw candles and lanterns glimmering within the pavilion. Even with the white ceiling and daylight still burning two hours before dusk, the interior of the pavilion had gathered shadows.

Dare squinted when he entered and saw that, indeed, a throne had been set up inside, and upon it sat Prince Darius's father, the King of Brookfall, looking a bit more haggard and gray than the last time Dare had seen him. It had only been a season, but if felt like years that he'd been away. Years since Prince Darius had died in his arms.

Sudden fear gripped Dare's arms and legs. For a moment he could not move deeper into the tent. Mal took a half-step and froze, glancing back at him.

This was it. In this one place, everything ended and began again. How it would end and how it would begin were the two unknowns that paralyzed Dare.

"Darius, come forward," came the king's voice.

His lungs shuddered. There wasn't enough air in here. Dare felt alone even with Mal not two steps away.

One of the guards outside the door and one step to the left of Dare, murmured in a low voice, "You will go down on one knee."

Both princes obeyed, though Dare saw Mal tense to be in such a vulnerable position in this brutal moment.

Without stepping over the threshold, the guard announced them.

"Your Highness, Prince Darius of Brookfall, and Prince Malory of Shastan."

After the announcement, the flap to the tent closed. Mal and Dare were alone to face the king.

Dare bowed his head. But through his fallen locks, he saw the king stand and take a step forward. A man at his side, obviously Lord Brandon, followed.

Lord Brandon was a tall man in his early forties, still handsome, with short graying hair and scar at his chin as if once in his youth the skin had been bisected. This formidable-looking man was a stranger to Dare.

The king said one word. "Darius! You married one of them? How could you?"

Dare heard a rush of blood in his ears.

"Stand, my son!"

Dare knew the king to be a cold and stoic man who held little love for his son. Their relationship was based more on blood and on loyalty to blood. The heart had never come into it. It had made Darius surly but he'd never cried over it. All of that was why this set up might work.

Dare stood. He lifted his chin. He met the gaze of the old king.

The king of Brookfall looked him up and down. "That is *not* my son!"

"Sire," said Mal in a low, fast voice. "He is Prince Darius's double, here on the prince's command."

Dare made a motion with his hand at the still-kneeling Mal to quiet.

"I asked to see my son!"

"Sire," Dare began. "You do remember me."

The muscles about the king's eyes tightened. "Of course I remember you. My son the prince's servant. You are Dare. I have known you since you were born." He mumbled unintelligibly under his breath. His eyes shone bright for a moment. His brows lowered. "I thought you had been killed."

Dare said, keeping his voice firmly in control. "Prince Darius and I were spared when he was taken. I was taken along with him. If communications to you failed to mention that, it is undoubtedly because I am a servant not worth mentioning."

"Where is my son!"

"He's here. I swear it. Just beyond the border. Within eyesight, Sire."

"Why did he send you?"

"He always sent me to do his work," Dare replied. "You taught him this strategy. He always does meetings this way. Always."

"This is true. But never in meetings with me. Never!" The king's face reddened. The muscles of his cheeks tightened with fury. "This is an outrage and you both know it. You must call his guards and have him approach this tent immediately!"

Dare made no move. Mal still knelt on one knee, silent. But his golden head was up and alert.

Dare said, "Your son—Prince Darius—fears for his very life. He cannot easily trust. You know this, you raised him, after all. He has doubles for tense occasions such as this one."

"Do you think I'm an idiot?" the king roared. "If I, the king, cannot meet my own son, how can I be assured of his health and well-being?"

"I am his husband." Mal spoke up. "I give you my word. He is quite well."

"I don't believe it!" The king's hands became fists. "He would never have married an enemy prince. He would never have agreed to such traitorous vows."

"He would to save his own life," said Mal. "And now he lives. I guarantee it."

Dare watched as Mal faced the king. Mal was trembling but only in such a way that Dare noticed. It was in the edges of his hands where they rested on his thighs. And a throbbing vein along the side of his throat.

"To save his life?" the king asked. "Then he is still a prisoner and not consigned to his own free will?"

"By his will," Dare said to the king, "Prince Darius will not see you. But you can see him, safe under guard, just where the clover meadow begins on the Shastan side of the border."

"This is a trick. You will have him brought here at once!" The king's fists balled and he lifted them as if to show strength when really he looked like a shaky old man.

Dare and Mal exchanged quick looks.

"If you will but look outside you can see him," Dare said. "He is afraid to come closer. You know this about him. His paranoia will not allow him—"

"You, a mere servant, you cannot tell me about my son! About his fears. He has never been afraid to come to me, and he will come. Now! This is my command! You will go and get him and bring him to me!"

The tone of voice came out not only as an order, but like a threat. And it was loud. Dare could only hope his and Mal's own guards standing beyond the awning about ten paces away from the entrance would not overhear the king calling Dare a servant.

In this precise moment, even with the angry king accusing him of lying, Dare still had hope they could pull this charade off. If only he could convince him that Darius was alive and simply did not want to see him.

The candles flickered. The shadows on the insides of the pavilion were like a gray wave held back. As if time itself did not breathe.

The king strode to the entrance where the ribbons on the interior silk curtains were tied back by dark ropes against the canvas flap had been let down for privacy. He called, "Guard!"

Dare turned to watch him, but was distracted when Lord Brandon came from behind the throne toward Mal.

Mal did not move.

74

Lord Brandon came forward. His hands had been in his robes. Now they came into sight and something flashed. Not jewelry.

Lord Brandon had a knife. A small one, to be sure, but with at least a four inch blade. Enough to do damage.

"Guard!" yelled the king.

"Mal," yelled Dare.

At that same moment, Mal stood and in one sweeping motion caught Lord Brandon's arm in a chop, avoiding a knife-thrust and almost managing to knock Brandon down. But Lord Brandon was stronger and quicker than he looked, even in heavy robes, and he backed off with the knife at ready again against Malory who was unarmed.

"No!" Dare cried out. "Sire! It's an act of war to draw on a prince!"

"Show me my son," said the king in a too-quiet voice.

He seemed unconcerned that his advisor was attacking Mal, as if he wanted it to happen. At his command, the outside door guards opened the tent flap and checked that the pretty red curtain was secure. In the meantime, Mal and Lord Brandon were circling each other through the tent shadows.

"Show me my son and then Lord Brandon will stand down," said the king. "It is only fair, since my son is being held captive still, and away from my sight, that I secure the son of Shastan. The insult of only your arrival, Dare, is grave. Both you and he should know this."

Mal and Brandon continued to circle each other.

"He's right there. He's afraid." Dare heard the pleading in his voice as he pointed toward the knoll. "He was afraid of this very thing happening which was why he wouldn't come and sent me in his stead. As he always does."

"Then he sent his husband to his death. Knowingly. There must not be much love lost between them." The king's voice was tuneless, cold.

"You must believe me. He willingly married Prince Malory." Dare came up alongside the king. "Please!"

"I know my own son. I imagine this was forced upon him."

"Look." Now Dare could see out the front opening. Verick stood surrounded by a troop of five armored guards. "He's just over there. Your son the prince is fine. But he is afraid to cross the border."

The king peered out, squinting. His guards had their hands on their sword handles, ready to draw at his command.

"That is not my son."

"Of course it is!"

But as Dare looked, Verick, who at first had been too far away but brought closer on Mal's command, was now too close. His head was turned. The king would be able to see a line of dark hair along the edge of the cloak's hood, and his stance, which was straight but far from proud and princely.

Verick was the right height and build, but he then he made the mistake of looking at one of the guards, as if he'd been spoken to. And his head turned just enough to see him smile. A smile given to a mere guard.

Prince Darius never smiled. Especially not at guards.

Dare felt all the blood drain from his face.

"That is *not* my son!"

"It is…" Dare began, but lost his voice.

He had never been ready for this meeting.

Now he faced a king he'd grown up knowing, if only through cool glances of appraisal or disapproval in relation to Prince Darius, Dare's own needs set aside. For he had been only the servant all along.

It was instinct for him to want to bend at the neck and shoulders, look at the ground, hands behind his back. Eye contact with a king when one was a lowly servant was dangerous. Outside of normal protocols. You might be whipped for it. But this was not normal. And when he'd been little, before he knew protocols, he always greeted the king as he would any person who entered his view.

Now the king looked at him, his dark eyes commanding.

Dare not look away. "What have you done? Dare, the one I trusted to see to my son's welfare for his entire life. What have you done to my son?"

"I have not—"

"Leave him be!" came Mal's voice from the left.

He and Lord Brandon had stopped circling each other. Mal had his hands up, braced for a knife attack. Lord Brandon made no move, but it was obvious he was carefully listening to the exchange between Dare and the king.

"Your son is out there and safe. He does not want to see you. It could not be more obvious. Would you start a war over the eccentricities of a nineteen year old boy? This is ridiculous," Mal said.

"That is not my son out there!" repeated the king.

"Tell your hired sword to lower his knife!" Mal said in a commanding tone. "This is *not* why we came here, to be treated like this, to start a fight!"

"That is not Darius!" The king glared, placing a heavy hand on Dare's shoulder. "Where is he? I want you to tell me. You, Dare. What happened? And where is my son?" The fingers clenched against muscle just enough to pinch with a promise of pain if Dare did not answer correctly.

"He has not been well—"

"No lies!"

The hand on Dare's shoulder tightened.

"I'm not—"

"Then I want to see him. You will take me to my son. We will each have the same number of guards. We will go together. The enemy prince stays here with Lord Brandon."

"No," Mal said.

Dare shook his head. "I made an oath to your son to take his place." This was not, technically, a lie.

"I don't care about oaths to my son. I am king. My will supersedes any oath."

Dare might have played the prince a hundred times in his life, and this last time for a period of months among strangers, but his body quivered at his king's command. The father of Prince Darius had been a distant and absent parent, someone who ignored Darius's conditions as if they did not matter, as if Dare substituting for the prince at any given moment did not matter. But he was still king. He held all the power. Dare's body withered under that stare. He thought he might break apart.

Mal said, "If we even begin to approach, Prince Darius runs."

"Not," said the king, "if you tell your guards to hold him still."

Dare took a deep breath. He heard Mal say again, "Lower your knife!"

He heard the king say, "Guard!"

One more time, Mal commanded. "Lower your knife!"

Dare saw no answering response from Lord Brandon.

Guards fought to reach the pavilion entryway as the king yelled for them again.

At the same time, Dare heard Mal yell, "Protect the princes!"

More voices down the line of the king's guard sounded, and a strange answering response from his and Mal's own guard replied in the form of yells.

This was now completely out of control. This was not how it was supposed to happen.

Dare gasped when he looked out the tent's opening and saw men draw their swords. Across the fields, silver flashed in the low, bronze sunlight. Metal upon metal scraped as scabbards were emptied and naked blades met the air.

The king's hand on Dare's shoulder clenched hard and he brought Dare closer to him.

"Prince Malory!" The king's head was raised. He was not addressing Dare at all anymore. "You will take me to my real son. No more imposters! You will order your men to stand down. Or I will order my guards to kill you, Dare, and everyone on this field."

Dare said, "No! You can't!" It would be war. All he had done would have been for nothing.

The king held his free hand up in sight of the guards at the entry. In that moment, Dare saw his only way out. A vulnerability that in seconds would be gone.

Bowing his head, he charged the king.

Chapter Ten

Dare could only give attention with part of his mind to Mal as he heard the tussle, the thumps of muscle hitting muscle, the tearing of clothing, the grunt of pain as – maybe – a knife silently sliced at flesh.

His own fight was for his life and the king, though long past his prime, was still strong for an old, rattled man.

He pushed the king away, coming in deep with his free shoulder and hitting him in the chest, turning his body to free himself from the king's grip as they both lost their balance and fell to the rug.

Despite Dare's attempt to stop the king's command for battle, the guards had already seen too much.

Outside, men shouted, horses thundered, and the ringing of battle stung the air. Sword hit sword. He saw it all in a flash, but now all his attention was on the man beneath him. Darius's father. A man who had never been a father to him or Darius, but who had been in his life since he was an infant. The King of Brookfall.

Dare couldn't think beyond his next move. All sound dimmed. Light faltered.

The king pushed up with his fists. But Dare had everything to lose and felt himself gain added strength with his resolve. With his knee, Dare pressed hard into the king's chest.

The tent sides seem to close in, but he did not relent. Something was happening to him. He pressed down hard as the king pummeled him with his fists. Dare felt nothing. Thought nothing. Kept pushing, his knee going down to hold the torso in place, his entire weight upon it.

The king yelled, but the sound seemed not to reach Dare's ears. Distantly, he saw shadows coming together and breaking apart in another part of the tent. Mal and Lord Brandon.

He continued to kneel, the king's blows bouncing off him as if from a child, no strength or effort behind them. Then the king grabbed upward and placed his large hands about Dare's neck.

Time went hushed about him. He saw again the brightness of the day, the horses peacefully grazing amongst clover and dandelions, and smelled the homey scent of campfires along the border.

Time needed to stop and return to that moment. He felt it almost accomplish that impossible task.

As he looked down into the king's slowly reddening eyes, he stepped into a new realm. And watched him draw labored breath after breath.

Everything around Dare darkened and he realized his own breathing began to hitch. The strong fingers around his throat dug into muscle and tendon, blocking his windpipe.

He thought he heard Mal yelling again but could not make out the words. He wanted to answer. To let him know he was all right and shouldn't worry. But things were not all right.

The world topsy-turvied. All wrong. A red fog seemed to come up from the ground. Or was that the ceiling of the pavilion draped in silk? But the silk was on the outside, not the inside. Was it falling? Were they going to be trampled by the fighting men and horses beyond its walls?

Something hit the back of his head. Hard.

The king was on top of him now, eyes wide but unmoving. He made a strangled sound, words forming a partial sentence. "...never be my son..."

Dare tried to push him off, but the fingers against this throat did not budge.

Something dark and angular, with a deep curve, rose up behind the king. An object much like a tankard, or pitcher.

It came toward Dare. Lower and lower. But instead of striking him, it struck the king.

It was the last thing Dare saw before reality vanished.

*

Dare woke to shouting and an acrid taste in his mouth.

He blinked away the blackness that still invaded his vision. His throat ached. He coughed hard.

A body lay next to him.

Dare sat up. "Mal?"

He realized his hands were tied behind his back, and his ankles wrapped tight with rope.

He stared with dread at the unmoving man beside him. Lean and tall, wearing the royal cloak, his gray hair thin, receding.

The king was dead.

For a moment, Dare thought, *I killed him.*

Then he realized, along with the purple bruise marks on the king's neck, a dark crust had formed on and around his left ear. Dried blood. And he remembered the object coming toward him. He had expected a blow to his own head. Instead, it hit the king. Someone had struck the king.

He was still inside the royal pavilion. Miraculously, the tent remained standing. But there was no sign of Mal. Or Lord Brandon.

Dare's heart thumped in his chest. He strained to hear anything from outside. He couldn't see past the front entrance. The flap had fallen, or been deliberately closed.

The sounds that stood out were distant yells, occasional hoof beats on grass or dirt, and the gong-like clanging of metal on metal also faraway. Mostly, there was silence close by and all around him. Which felt as threatening to him as an all-out fight.

Wherever Mal had gone, it could not be good. Dare saw bright spots of blood on the pavilion rug leading to the entrance, fresh blood still red as new dawn dying the wool fibers with its horrific brilliance.

Dare had seen so much blood when he'd first been taken by men from Shastan. When Prince Darius had died in his arms. But that did not mean he was used to it. It repulsed him. Made his body tense into a panic worse than facing mad kings and dungeon masters.

He turned over onto his knees and tried, with his hands tight behind his back, to shuffle his body toward the entrance. He kept falling, flopping onto his shoulders and face. He pushed hard with his bound feet, inching himself forward. Avoiding the blood stains as best he could, as well as the corpse of the king.

Something like a great wind seemed to draw up outside the tent. Then he heard horses snort, hooves pound. Shouts. Broken cries. Leather on metal. Ringing like bells, not swords.

The tent flap opened. A rush of armored men streamed in, circling Dare who lay on his side looking up. Looking for Mal.

The men who gazed back were Brookfall guardsmen with the blackbird insignia on a red background emblazoned on their cloaks and shields. Those who still had cloaks and shields. Most of their armor was covered in mud and blood.

The double line up of men extended all the way out the door. Dare could not see beyond them but guessed the line kept going. It parted in the middle, bodies framing the door, allowing a path between them. On that path, Lord Brandon came, pulling Mal by a blood-encrusted chain. Behind them, half a dozen men dressed as lords and council members followed.

Dare caught his breath at the sight of Mal. Armor gone. White shirt ripped in the back and front. He had a long gash across his chest, still dripping blood. At his left knee, his trousers gaped from another slash, and more blood welled.

About his mouth was a thick scarf pulled taut like a horse's bit.

Dare recognized none of the lords. But they were obviously a newer retinue of the old king, now led by Lord Brandon. A new council since the short time he'd been missing? Why?

"For all to see, the king is dead," Lord Brandon pronounced.

After some shifting and mumbling and a few outcries of grief, one of the lords said, "Why is the heir bound?"

Lord Brandon, who had not a hair or piece of clothing out of place despite having fought against Malory, replied. "They came in together to do harm to the king."

The guard in front who stood taller than the rest, his blond hair damp against his brow, his armor spattered with mud and blood, said, "The king his dead. Who has murdered the king?"

Lord Brandon looked over the guards and the lords and raised his voice. "The king is murdered by the enemy prince, Prince Malory of Shastan."

Mal's curses could be heard even through the binding at his mouth. He shook his head in denial. His shock-darkened eyes sought out Dare.

No one else could see that look and know. No one knew Mal the way Dare did now. He saw only horror there in the eyes of his lover, and apology. Apology to Dare that everything had gone wrong. But Dare could not be sure Mal had not been the one to kill the king. If Mal thought Dare's life was in danger, he would have killed. But right now Mal was shaking his head in denial.

There was one only other person inside the royal pavilion when the tussling began, and when the king had commanded the guards outside to attack the enemy.

Dare swung his gaze to Lord Brandon. He remembered the hard tankard coming toward him. He had thought it was Lord Brandon's hand, that the tankard had been directed at him. He believed in that moment that he would finally die and leave this nightmare forever.

But he could see now that the tankard had been intended for the king alone. But had the arm that had raised it belonged to the king's own second hand?

Lord Brandon knew the truth of Dare. He'd heard it played out, the king's recognition of Dare as a mere servant, the king's command that Dare take him to his son. But no one else had heard.

Now Lord Brandon was pretending Dare was the heir? But why?

"If Prince Darius did not kill him, then he is the new king. He must be unbound at once!" said another lord.

Another piped up. "He is heir to the throne. He must be allowed to stand and state his piece!"

"A full trial is in order," said Lord Brandon. "He will be allowed to speak then and only then before all. I am the Lord Viceroy for the king. And my decision on this matter is final."

Dare saw Lord Brandon glance at the tall blond guard. The guard gave a slight nod. He would back the Lord Viceroy, and not Dare. If he was the guard in charge, his men would follow him.

Of course Dare knew instantly why the look was given. Dare could not be allowed to stand free, or even to go to the court at Castle Brookfall. Too many living in the castle would recognize him as an imposter. Dozens there knew him on sight as Prince Darius's companion and servant.

How long had Dare been unconscious? It had been at least long enough for Brandon to make plans behind everyone's back. New plans, for no one could have foreseen that the real Prince Darius would not have come to meet his own father. Not even Lord Brandon.

And, Dare wondered, where had he taken Mal during that time?

Dare wanted to speak up but kept his mouth shut. He was the official heir for right now, but was unsure how to proceed until he had more information.

Mal stood, hands manacled, neck chained, dripping blood onto the rug. He looked pale but still strong of mind. His eyes told Dare to sit tight.

"The enemy has retreated for now," Lord Brandon said. "We will all re-group at Castle Brookfall."

Dare's chest tightened even more through his impossible stress. He knew he would not be allowed to arrive home alive. He and Mal both could not be allowed to live. Not if Lord Brandon was calling the shots. And most especially not if Lord Brandon had been the actual murderer of the king.

Since Brandon could not kill them outright, he would make sure their deaths looked provoked. Or like accidents.

"See to the wounded and break the rest of the camp. The healthiest of us will start for home right away. The rest will follow when they can." He barked his orders as if he were already king. "Bring my horse. Split the provisions. The king's guard shall ride with me and the prisoners."

No one protested. No one argued. All obeyed.

When the men left to ready everything for the journey, only Dare, Mal and Lord Brandon were left in the tent with guards flanking the doorway a few feet away.

Lord Brandon glared down at Dare, who sat with his hands and feet bound on the rug.

"Say one word and I will have Prince Malory's head on a stick faster than you can blink and no one here will care to stop me."

Chapter Eleven

Dusk had come and gone. A large contingent of armed guards had left hours ahead of them, and Dare figured it was to break the news of the king's death and keep the peace as the people reacted in fear and grief.

The sick and wounded stayed behind. The rest of them, including Dare and Mal, rode by night as if Lord Brandon was in a hurry himself to return to the castle.

The sky overhead prickled with stars. The moon, at the quarter-mark, peered blind and voiceless from its wine-dark vantage.

Dare had not been treated too badly. The bindings about his ankles had been taken off. But his wrists were shackled with metal, now, like Mal's.

The horse that carried Mal rode to the left and behind him. He had not been treated for his cuts. He had not been given anything to drink or eat. He had been thrown over the saddle and tied down. Dare's pulse pounded to see him like that, and he begged for lenience. His words fell on unconcerned ears.

If these men thought Dare was the rightful king, there had to be something he could do. But they also thought he'd committed patricide by proxy in collusion with the Shastan prince. In which case, if he was found guilty, his claim to the throne was negated.

Brandon was keeping their secret for a reason.

Dare knew that now. He'd seen the carnage as they left the border encampment. He had nearly broken down when he saw Verick's body in the grass among too many other Shastans, including other helpless servants.

Brandon had killed the king of Brookfall. It had to be. There was no other reason for his duplicity with his own men.

And he'd had Verick killed, that was apparent. He wanted Dare's and Mal's secret kept so he could officially try and convict them and take power for himself.

What had been going on in Brookfall in the few months since he'd left? For this was no impulsive, unplanned coup. Had the entire kingdom been thrown into unrest after the kidnapping of Prince Darius? Was Dare then responsible?

His eyes blurred as they rode through dimly moonlit fields and crossed black rushing brooks that chattered in uncaring voices.

The men in armor were noisy as they rode, clanking enough to wake the dead. Horses snorted, unhappy about having no bedtime. Some whinnied up and down the lines, calling to each other in their discomfort.

Mal never made a sound. Dare was almost ashamed to be more worried about him than kings and kingdoms and tired horses. But Mal was his life now, his heart. Without him, everything would be worthless.

Dare had only newly turned nineteen. He knew little of kingships, or how to use one to fight battles and gain power. Lord Brandon now knew this.

But Dare did know about princes. And how to be one. How others automatically revered and respected them, even if they did not like them. How they had rushed to obey Prince Darius's order back at the castle as he was growing up, even if Darius was awful to the servants and the other lords and ladies his own age. He knew how to play the part, to speak, and often watched in amazement as people took his words on faith alone, unquestioning.

But this council under Lord Brandon was new. They had never met Prince Darius and didn't trust Dare now. They had no reason to mistrust the man who apparently led them, Lord Brandon, now that their true king was dead.

But if he was going to do anything to help Mal, he needed to buck up, muster the courage, not act the role, but *be* the role of heir to Brookfall, and its rightful king.

He never wanted to be a real prince, despite enjoying the social role at times in his youth. But to be a king? Mal had said it could happen. All along as he played the role of prince, he had never wanted the reality for himself.

Before, he needed to play the prince in an enemy kingdom to save his very life and prevent a war. But now he needed to be the king. To save Mal. And if war had already started, at the very least he could stop it from escalating.

They rode all night, stopping only once to rest the horses and eat a small meal.

During their break, guards grabbed Mal from his horse and threw him to the ground. He did not move.

Under close scrutiny from Lord Brandon's personal guards, Dare could do nothing.

Finally, after many long minutes of silence, Mal groaned.

Dare said, "Let me go to him. He needs water."

The guards ignored him.

Dare was separated from the main group. Guards brought him a plate of dried meat, cheese and a roll. They left a skin of water. He ate with his bound hands, slowly. And watched Mal where he lay.

Dare kept trying to get the attention of the guard nearest to him, the big blond and commander of the king's guard. The one who looked tough, always frowning.

"Please," he said when he caught the guard's eye. "Let me give him some bites of my own meal. And some water."

He glanced at Mal who lay as if dozing in the broken flowers of the meadow amidst the dust raised by the horses' hooves. The air was made of flowing black shadows. But he could still see the black stain on Mal's shirt at his chest. And the stiff fabric of his trousers stuck to the skin of his injured knee. The caked blood of his injuries. If they weren't treated, they could fester.

"Please," Dare said. "Let me go to him."

The guard said, "You are not to approach him."

A sting of anger burned through his veins. "I am the rightful heir. I demand it."

The guard laughed.

"Bring Lord Brandon to me at once!" Dare insisted.

"He has better things to do right now than talk to you."

"I am the king now, and when I am crowned, you will be rewarded if you help me."

"You don't look like a king. And you are a prisoner at this moment."

"This is Lord Brandon's doing! Do you not understand? He's the one who—"

"What is going on here?" From the shadows behind them, a strong voice called out. Lord Brandon came into the clearing, the moonlight highlighting his angular features, and creating a seam of light in his straight, dark hair.

"I gave explicit instruction not to talk to the prisoner!" Brandon said.

"Sir, I wish only to see that Mal has something to drink and eat," Dare said. "He can have my food. And his wounds need to be treated and bound. Or he might not make it to the castle." He didn't add that he suspected Lord Brandon and his guard didn't want them to make it to the castle alive.

Brandon shifted his gaze to Mal's prone body. Mal's shoulders rose and fell, showing he was breathing at least. He might have been sleeping or unconscious. Either way, it did not look good.

Brandon said, "He'll make it. His wounds are superficial. I checked them myself."

The answer surprised Dare. Brandon had to be lying.

"He needs water at the very least," Dare demanded. Then lower, "You can't do this. He's a prince."

"Can't I? How well did Shastan treat you?"

Dare pressed his lips tight.

"That well, eh? Until you married the crown prince." He lowered his voice so the guards would not hear and leaned in. "Was that your plan?"

Shocked at the statement, Dare tried to get his thoughts under control. This man was too easily taking charge of everything. "And while Darius… While I was gone, what was your plan? With the king. With *my* father?"

"Your father?" He chuckled. He bent low and whispered into Dare's ear. "You keep playing the role, yes, by all means. It only makes everything easier for me."

"I could tell the truth," Dare ventured. He glanced at the blond guard to see if he heard. But the guard stared out at the field, at nothing, staying out of it.

"You do that and your kingdom still falls, and I am still the next in line after no heirs are left alive. Right now, you benefit more from staying your course."

"You mean you benefit more," Dare replied.

But he knew he was trapped. It was better to hold onto pretend power than a servant's handful of nothing. He'd be executed much quicker as a servant. As the king's heir, at least he had a voice.

"What did happen after the prince's party was ambushed and killed?" Dare asked.

"What happened when you yourself were ambushed? Did you assist in killing the prince?"

"Most certainly not! But you… you had plans, didn't you? It was the perfect time to move in after the prince's party was ambushed."

Brandon gave him a sly smile. His eyelids closed halfway. "The king was already mad. He went a little madder. There was a coup in the council. I stepped up. You don't know my name, do you?"

Dare shook his head.

"That is because the king was paranoid, just like the son. He sent all blood relatives far away, some banished forever, trusting no one who might have any hint of a legitimate claim to the throne if he were gone. All this was right before you were born. Before the prince. I'm the king's nephew. I grew up in the palace. Before Prince Darius was born, the king sent everyone away, including my father, the king's brother. But now, with my father dead, and the king dead, I am the rightful heir to the throne. And you, a mere servant," he said the word *servant* as if he were spitting it, "are in my way."

Dare blinked. A blood relative. He had not known the king of Brookfall had anyone but Darius as immediate family.

His mind swam with possibilities. Brandon had come after Darius who was thought to be imprisoned. He'd no doubt been looking for opportunity; who wouldn't in this unsettling arena?

At the border, Brandon had found his perfect scapegoats for regicide. Mal and Dare. If Brandon had not found out his secret he might not have seen it as the perfect opportunity. But now he knew.

Brandon could tell Dare's secret to all and be vindicated, but he needed to lay blame for the murder of a king and go through a real trial to see perfect justice, his heir to the throne unquestioned.

Dare's ruse set the perfect stage for Lord Brandon to succeed to the throne.

It all made perfect and terrible sense.

Dare kept watch on the dark-eyed gaze of the lord. "Why not just kill him outright, then?" He moved his chin in the direction of Mal, but his gaze never wavered from Brandon's face.

"Do you think me a monster? I don't kill princes. I am benevolent and a pacifist. Already the council and the court love me."

"You are not. You will still see us die."

Brandon's smile crooked at the edges into disgust. "By justice."

"No. Not justice. You killed the king." Dare's tone came out even, though he was shaking inside.

The blond guard moved slightly, as if Dare's statement had revealed something he had not considered.

92

"No. Your beloved did."

"That's what you want people to believe." Though he had not really seen the deed, had not made out the hand that crashed the tankard against the king's skull, he was sure of that now. Mal would have never done such a thing. He would have pulled the king off Dare, fought him, but he would not have deliberately killed him.

Brandon put his hand on the imprints along Dare's throat, where the bruising of the king's fingers still smarted.

"I thought he had already killed you," he said softly.

Dare backed away, glaring.

"Turns out," said Brandon, "it's no inconvenience at all. It helps my case. The two of you. Colluding. A servant with a prince. If, by some chance, the tribunal does not call for Prince Malory's head, he will surely lose it even if banished back to his own kingdom for his duplicity, his dishonor to his own king and father, his own queen the mother, and his people."

Dare thought if only he could explain, if the truth won out, he'd have sympathy and empathy on his side, and maybe the power to save Mal.

Brandon seemed to read his mind as he spoke one last proclamation. "Say nothing and I will keep you alive for a while. Maybe even spare you the chopping block. And your scheming princely lover. That will be harder, though. The people will want Mal's head for his regicide of their king. You might be in chains for the rest of your life, though, but you'd live."

Through gritted teeth, Dare said, "If you already have a mind to execute him after we arrive, then at least let me give him water."

Brandon's dark brows narrowed.

Dare added, "It will show them even more that you have compassion."

Brandon's lips pressed to a snarl. He turned to the blond guard. "Let him tend to the prince. No talking."

The guard nodded and came to Dare, waiting for him to gather up the food and water flask.

As Dare approached Mal, the back of his throat fluttered. The muscles there tightened. His eyes began to sting. He took a deep breath, holding back his fear, his grief.

Everything that could go wrong had gone wrong. He'd known it would. He should have come up with another plan. They should have run. Perhaps. Or told the truth to King Millard. At the very least, they'd be in Shastan still. Dare would be in chains, but he'd been there before. And survived.

Mal lay half on his side, his clothing torn and bloody, his hair a mass of tangled bronze knots and damp curls. Dare smelled the metal of dried blood, the acrid air of pain and fear.

When he touched Mal gently on the shoulder, Mal jerked and gave a small cry.

The guard stood over them, too close, smelling of horse and a held-back fury. Like the sickness of soured wine mixed with the rage of someone who has known only meanness and hardship.

Mal opened his eyes. "Dare." His voice was made of rocks.

The guard poked Mal hard on the side with his boot. "No talking!"

Mal's eyes sought Dare's. Dare shook his head. Put a gentle finger to Mal's lips. He had placed the food and water to the side, and grasped Mal's fingers with his free hand.

He swallowed hard. The trembling within him would not stop, but he breathed deep to control it. He gave Mal a soft smile.

He took his finger from Mal's lips and grasped the flask. Then he pushed his arm under Mal's shoulders and held him gently against his chest.

Mal gasped in pain but also relief as Dare put the water flask to his mouth. He drank greedily, water spilling over his chin and the sides of his mouth.

When Dare took the flask away, Mal mouthed silently, *More.*

He let Mal catch his breath, then gave him more water. Slowly, methodically, he dabbed at Mal's cuts with his own dampened cloak.

Mal winced.

He offered Mal bread and cheese. Mal turned away. Dare knew exactly how he felt, having once been a prisoner himself, sick on horseback, headed into enemy lands.

He offered more water, which Mal did take. Hands tied loosely in front of him, it was hard to maneuver. He used both hands to take the flask away when Mal began to choke. Then, Dare held Mal awkwardly. Mal's hands were bound, too, but behind his back. He had no balance or coordination. His weight lay entirely in Dare's lap.

Over several sessions of drinking and resting, Mal drank nearly the entire flask of water. Once, he choked. Dare had held him, both arms under one arm of Mal's, as close as he could, pressing his cheek into the coils and ravels of his hair.

In the cool, summer midnight, the warmth of Mal soaked through Dare's clothes and warmed his skin. The mists of the fields were like dreamy hands beckoning. *This way to safety. This way to the idyll wilds.*

But the truth reared between them. There was no escape.

The guard said, "Get up."

Dare had to let go. His love, his heart lying a wreck in the weeds. He had to leave him. For his own good. For them both. For now they might survive. At least a few more days.

Something Stix, the overly-talkative dungeon master in Shastan had said, rang in his ear. *Men in fear become savage.*

He would get nowhere in this state. He must quell his fear and think. Use his mind. He was among men who had only followed orders, and had no choice but to follow a new man. But they were still men. If Dare showed fear, he would only make them stronger. If he showed strength and poise, played his role, well, he knew from experience that most men, even guards under order, hesitated when it came to harming royalty.

None of us is any better in our suffering than others, Stix had said. Dare had not forgotten. These were lessons he'd always been learning when he sought so very hard not to hate Darius, or be caught up in his convoluted and lost-boy mind which had made him paranoid and often cruel. These were lessons he'd learned when he played the role of prince for him, forgetting his place sometimes, but never growing to resent it. Darius had not won out over him by virtue of being royal, or bullying. Dare had never stopped seeing a world of heart and beauty. Even in chains he saw the rainbow hues in rust.

Stix had talked a lot that night Dare had been whipped and brought to the extremes of pain again and again. Dare had not wanted to listen. But part of him had listened, for there was nothing to hang onto but words. That sedately calm voice. The voice of his tormentor who apologized for everything he did.

Stix had told him about men opening, changing, evolving, coming into new worlds and taking second and third chances. About re-making the self often through trials by fire.

If he made it to the castle alive, he would have to become a new man. He would have to play his role so well that even the servants who'd known him his whole life would question their eyes and believe what they were told. He was Darius. Prince of Brookfall. He was the rightful king. He was *not* an imposter. And he was innocent of all he was accused of.

As the guard impatiently nudged him with his foot, Dare let Mal down to into the weeds with as much gentleness as he could. He twisted his hands in his bindings and lifted them, brushing his palms against Mal's tight cheek, feeling the rasp of a day's growth of beard. He leaned down, placing a soft kiss to his forehead.

"Up!" croaked the guard.

Dare rose.

Out the corner of his eye, Dare saw two more guards approach Malory, pick him up and drag him to his horse.

He turned to the blond guard, all armor and gray shadows, eyes like pinpoints of light almost blotted out by duty and fear and a need to eat and fight and be important. Once there had been a little boy behind those eyes. Probably abused, but still a smiling cherub when he got his way.

As the guard clasped him hard at the elbow, steering him toward Midnight, Dare said, "I'm coming. You don't have to push."

"You are not moving fast enough."

Dare did not argue. Instead, he said, "What's your name?"

This seemed to through the guard off kilter for a moment.

"You have a name, right? I don't want to just say *hey you* to you."

"No tricks," the guard mumbled.

"It's not a trick."

Finally, after some moments, the guard said, "Andrus."

"Andrus. I'll remember your politeness to me about that. I'm Darius. Rightful heir to the throne of Brookfall."

Andrus grumbled, then said, "No talking!"

The guard was nervous and Dare understood nervousness. He'd been around it his whole life. Been around men with everything to lose. Men with agendas. Men with fear.

"All right, Andrus," he said quietly. "I won't talk anymore."

The guard said, "And don't think I don't know the truth. You are no more an heir than I am."

Dare's insides sagged at the bitter, unhappy words. But still, an unhappy guard was someone he could observe and maybe talk with again. Unhappiness was a vulnerability. Dare latched onto that, and it gave him a twinge of hope.

Chapter Twelve

It seemed an endless trek past darkened farms and tiny sleeping townships. The troops were not quiet as they went, and lanterns lit up windows and porches as they rode by fearful people not expecting an army to pass by in the night.

The rivers they rode alongside cast sylph-shadows over the land from dimly reflected moonlight and their own torch-men.

Lord Brandon led the parade. His horse seemed never to tire. *He* seemed never to tire.

Dare kept his head up and facing forward, but always he had one eye on Mal, again slung and tied over a horse's saddle, no doubt feeling every bump and sidestep like a lash from a whip on his sore body.

Dare remembered to keep breathing, deep and slow. Andrus rode beside him, tall and silent. It was no comfort. But Dare knew his name now. He'd only just begun to learn names. Later, he would learn the men's personalities.

The hours of early morning seemed thin, as if time pressed itself lightly upon this world and the next, mixing them. The sky was lightening to east in a greenish glow. Layer after layer of shadows came and went, first black, then brown and gray and golden where the flowers that had not yet been trampled raised their heads to the coming dawn.

Dare heard Mal sigh long and deep. It was almost a groan. Dare's heart swept up fast in worry, but he stayed steady. Already he was recognizing the landscape, fields that broke off into groves of olive trees where bright green jewelweed grew at their bases, used for medicinal purposes.

He did not know flora by experience, but he'd studied it from his prince's tutor. His education was not lacking. He'd been lucky in that. Thus, he could quite easily recognize the geography of their approach to home.

To Castle Brookfall.

*

By the time they reached the grand waterfalls in the valley, the castle had been in view for quite some time. Built by ancient kings on a rocky outcropping overlooking the valley and the farms, it had weathered well over the centuries. Its foundations ran deep into the mountain, fortifying it against erosion and earthquakes and howling winter winds.

The many turrets were dark points, like hollow arrows aimed at the sky. Blackbirds and doves flew about the coronets and the towers. Moss grew along the deep sides of marble slabs sunk deep into the mountain. It made the castle a mix of colors, blue, green and gray, like a dark jewel in the center of lush and gleaming lands.

A group of guards greeted the troop just beyond the waterfalls. "Hie! Who goes there?"

Lord Brandon answered in a voice of deep power. "Lord Brandon of the king's council. And our prisoners. Prince Darius. And Prince Malory of Shastan!"

"The king is dead! We have heard," yelled the head of the patrol. "The couriers came before dawn. We have taken the traitors you named to the courtyard and commenced executions."

Dare shivered. Executions? Traitors? Who might they be when Lord Brandon had only just himself murdered the king?

The patrol led the rest of the way to the castle, calling orders back and forth along the lines to keep them in order, and making everything look quite efficient. And official. Early morning swelled the sky pink and the sun over the mountains had gone from red to gold. The landscape was oblivious to the dramas of men, stretching beautifully in summer splendor.

The closer they got to the castle grounds, the more buildings Dare saw, houses, farmsteads, barns, and then the little towns that speckled the vast lands around the mountain, clusters of white and red and brown buildings where merchants resided and families lived.

In the early hours, there was already activity, but not the sort that Dare expected. He thought to see displays of wares and farmer's markets. Instead, he viewed people scurrying away, or coming forward to watch their approach. He saw a few wave. More, he saw, were in tears.

News of the king's death had apparently traveled fast.

Mal lay draped over his horse, too still. Wary eyes watched Dare from the sidelines. Dare's hands were tied at his wrists. Twice he heard someone say, "The prince!"

Of course these people would think him the prince, he who had doubled for Darius throughout their lives hundreds of times. He noted onlooker confusion. The confused looks came not from his identity, but the shackles he wore as he rode.

As they crossed the long, wooden bridge, narrowing to double file, the back of the group consisting of at least two hundred guards had to wait.

Dare was in front with Lord Brandon. He could see the grounds and the pathways, and the low-walled gardens, and the barns, the barracks and the outbuildings that surrounded the grand courtyard. All was the same as he remembered it.

Except for the screams. And the blood. And the dozens of bodies laid out on the cobblestones awaiting the death pyres.

He gasped at the atrocity. At more death. All these people could not be simple traitors to the king.

Most looked to be attired in servant garb, but some wore richer silks and brocades.

Bile rose in Dare's throat, acrid and bitter. His whole life had been sheltered because of Darius. Until the past few months when he'd seen more bloodshed than he'd ever imagined in his worst nightmares.

He still shivered at thoughts of Darius dying in his arms. And Verick, so young, so innocent, a man who loved horses and never did anyone any harm, slashed nearly in half and lying in the meadow.

Why were these people being butchered? But he already knew the answer. Because of him.

Softly, at his side, Brandon said, "Shocked?"

Dare shook his head, then whispered, "What happened?"

"These are all the people from the castle that knew Prince Darius growing up. And you. Now your identity is protected."

"All of them?" asked Dare, his voice rising.

"Do you not recognize any of them?"

But they were not close enough for Dare to see. He didn't want to see. He didn't want to be a part of this anymore. All of it, everything—the bloodshed, the horror, even the king's death—was because of him.

His resolve to save Mal rose up. He had to play his part a little longer. Buy Mal time. Do anything he could to save his life.

Dare put his shoulders back. Lifted his chin so that the cloak's hood fell just beyond his ears, showing his face. His hair pressed against his jaw line and tickled the back of his neck. His dark bangs flew up from his eyes in the burnt and death-smudged breeze.

He swallowed hard, as his throat threatened to close up. A single tear escaped, tracing a hot line down his cheek. Stinging. He felt flayed open. Vulnerable. As if all he had known was destroyed before his eyes and love would leave in a short moment.

He glanced once at Mal, still unmoving, and grit his teeth, moving on and into the courtyard.

Lord Brandon rode casually, with his own cloak, blood red, thrown back, the hood dangling behind him. As if the carnage meant nothing to him. As if none of this were real.

What kind of man…? Dare's mind started to ask. But he stopped himself abruptly. He knew. Darius. The king. Now the nephew. It seemed strange madnesses ran the genetic lines of this family. Or maybe the family line had a penchant for entirely skipping the process of acquiring a soul.

He tried not to look at the bodies as they passed, as the horses snorted and shied, their eyes rolling to show the whites. If he looked he knew he would pass out or be sick. Or start to sob and never be able to stop. He cared too much to look. Later, maybe if he asked for it, Brandon would give him a list of their names.

To escape more death and pain, Dare would give Lord Brandon the throne outright, but that would mean revealing his true identity to the public and now Brandon seemed to like keeping that secret. He wanted to take Dare down in front of the court *as* Prince Darius to show that his own legitimacy would never be questioned.

"If you say one word about it," he told Dare, "your lover's life is forfeit."

Husband. Dare wanted to correct him. *He's my husband!*

Walking up the steps and through the front entrance of the castle was as familiar to him as air. The moss and ivy-covered outer walls. The bitter scent of candles. Dragon sculptures lining the main hall. He remembered only him and Darius of all the palace children had been allowed to climb them when they were little. They were slippery. He thought he saw an old scuff mark toward the back of one sculpture, left there by tiny boots.

Servants stood along the bare, unadorned wall to the left, all bowing low, all strangers to Dare. He recognized not a one.

After riding all night, everyone in the party was tired. They had seen battle. None of them had properly rested.

Dare felt groggy, but kept his chin lifted. Walking behind Lord Brandon, his hands in shackles, he said, "The prince needs healers."

He turned to look behind him but could not see if Mal had been brought into the castle, or taken somewhere else.

"There will be time for rest for all. You will be taken to your old room. Under guard. Tomorrow the council will meet. Plans will be made. For your trial. And the prince's." Lord Brandon spoke *sotto voce*, pitched so only Dare could hear him.

"Please let him stay with me," said Dare, pleading. "Under guard. Nothing will happen, I swear it."

"That is not possible." Brandon dismissed him with a raised hand and moved off down another corridor, leaving Dare to be escorted by guards up the front, marble stairs to the prince's rooms, Darius's abode and the only home Dare had ever known.

Wherever they took Mal, Dare could not know. He hoped it wasn't the dungeon he and Darius had glimpsed as children when they'd climbed the wall and spied upon the forbidden prison. He felt his edge slipping again. If Mal was mistreated in his condition—

Dare did not want to think about it. He couldn't. He had to assume that Mal would be all right. Mal was strong. Quick. Smart. Not the sort that needed rescuing. No. Not that sort at all.

Dare felt as if he were the one who had been rescued. Again and again by Mal.

He knew the way to his old rooms blind. He didn't have to look. He didn't have to follow. But guards surrounded him. Right. Left. Front. Back. Their armor rattled too loud. They stunk of sweat and horse. They were faceless. Nameless. Except for Andrus who pushed him hardest of all.

"Quicker!" he said, when Dare stumbled. "Walk!"

When he got to the prince's rooms and entered, it felt and looked as if he'd left only yesterday. Nothing had changed. Servants had cleaned and made the bed. That was all.

Both his and Darius's lesson books still sat on the desk, neatly stacked beside quills and ink bottles and blotters. On the main table sat a ruby glass pitcher, and empty pewter plates with birds carved in relief on the edges. There was a stack of linen napkins, and fancy wine chalices trimmed in gold. A wooden bowl of fresh fruit sat in the center.

He wasn't hungry at all, but as the guards behind him entered, servants followed carrying more food.

"You may have a bath. Under guard," said Andrus.

Dare looked at his manacled hands, then up at the guard. "I won't be able to do much." He made his tone clipped, fighting his tiredness.

I'm a prince. I must act like a prince.

He wanted to say, *Lord Brandon killed the king.* But if he did, Mal's head would be on a post by morning.

"You can move your hands enough. A servant will wash your back. You'll make due," said Andrus.

"As prince of this land and rightful king, I'm sure I will."

At his burst of words, Dare noticed the guards behind Andrus straighten a bit. Two glanced at each other as if suddenly nervous. That was how he confirmed they did not find much comfort in going against a prince, even if they thought that prince had killed his own father.

When Dare removed his cloak, the impressions from the guards became even more nervous. He heard armor shift and breaths taken in almost fast enough to sound like gasps.

"Sir," said a male servant, bowing low to Andrus. "There is severe bruising around his throat. May I call on a healer?"

"You may not," Andrus said. But through is helm, which he still wore, he stared at the bruises which Dare could not see.

"Then I ask, sir, that I retrieve an ointment from the stores which might help the bruising heal." The servant had a fierce look on his face, and Dare ached at the thought of his loyalty being so misused.

"Yes. Go."

So, Dare was to be treated well. Almost pampered, but not quite.

Quickly, in the alcove near the water closet, the remaining servants prepared a bath in a metal tub. Two guards stood inside the room on either side of the door. Dare could see, as the servant retreated, that at least four more were stationed outside in the hall. Andrus stood in the center of the room, surveying all, giving orders, watching Dare closely.

Dare wondered what Andrus thought he might do, manacled as he was. But Andrus stepped forward, then, an iron key in hand. He made a motion for Dare to hold out his arms. Then he unlocked the manacles.

"I thought you were going to leave them," Dare said.

"I changed my mind." He paused as if expecting Dare to challenge him, then continued. "After your bath they will go back on. This way your clothing won't have to be torn from your body."

Dare balked but covered his shock with a practiced smirk. He knew how to act like the real Darius. "That is a relief. It's such a shame to spoil good clothing. The cloth merchants are slow this time of year due to the extra heat which impedes travel."

Andrus turned away from his commentary. "There will be less talk!"

"I am the prince. I'll talk all I want!"

Dare didn't look to see if Andrus turned to give him another glare. Instead, he walked calmly toward the tub, undoing his shirt as he went. Three servants met him, their hands reaching out to assist him. He stopped. He was used to this. He could do this. He held out his hands and allowed them to undress him.

When Dare had first seen Mal, he had thought him another spoiled prince. But Mal had hated being waited upon back at the Shastan Palace. He endured it as if it were a chore, and often sent them away to finish his own dressing and accessorizing himself.

Darius had loved the servants fawning over him, and ordered them about as if they were dogs, bullying them, making them do unnecessary tasks like re-polish already polished shoes. Worse, he made them undress and attend him naked while he bathed or dressed, embarrassing them. He made them do other chores that Dare did not do, like dusting and sweeping, all unclothed, until they were sweating all over. Then he would smack them on their buttocks, leaving red welts.

Dare bowed his head. Some memories were not worth focusing on.

Stripped now, his boots taken away to be cleaned, Dare sat in the steamy water, barely feeling it as it soaked his tired body. He was too worried about Mal to take any pleasure right now. His body wanted sleep badly, but he knew he would toss and turn and never be comfortable even after such a nice, warm bath.

Now that his hands were free, he could use the soaps that were offered to him. He bathed himself, but one of the male servants did see to his back.

After he rinsed and warm water was poured over his soapy head, shoulders and chest, a servant toweled his hair as he still lounged in the cooling water. Another, the one who'd gone for the ointment, gently applied it to his throat.

He had not realized how bad his injury there was until he felt the pressure of the man's fingers. There were places his skin was raw, and the oil stung. The bruising was a soreness and the muscles cringed to be touched.

The king had come close to killing him. Lord Brandon had saved his life. The incongruity of that was not lost on him.

He rose from the bath uncaring about his nudity. He'd been naked in front of servants his whole life. He'd played the naked servant to Prince Darius's whims.

His damp hair cooled his nape and tempered the hot skin where the ends trickled water against his shoulders. The salve on his bruises smelled of grass and jewelweed, the wild stuff he'd only just seen growing by the olive groves.

He thought of Mal again, perhaps thrown into a dungeon of straw bedding, left to rot. His breath hitched. He clamped down on the warmth behind his eyelids.

A servant slid his arms into a robe, fastening it for him in front. Andrus came forward then, manacles out.

Dare raised his arms, turning his head to the side as if uncaring.

"I slept with a collar and chain for weeks in Shastan. You think I care about these?" He rolled his shoulders back, narrowed his brows. He did not look at Andrus when he added, "Are you going to stand over me while I sleep?"

"You have killed your own father. You have slept with the enemy. You don't get to talk!" Andrus was perpetuating the lie. He'd overheard all Dare's secrets revealed. His loyalty to Lord Brandon seemed unbending.

"I have not yet stood trial. I am the rightful heir. I do as I please."

Andrus stepped forward and swung, smacking Dare hard across the face.

"I don't care what you are. Your father spoiled you. And you repay him by killing him. You do not speak again, or I *will* whip you!"

"You're very convincing." But Dare meant the lies, the words; he actually believed Andrus would whip him if given enough provocation. Lord Brandon would probably laugh at the spectacle.

Without a word, Dare walked to the bed which the servants had kindly turned down for him. He lay back upon the blankets and pillows, still in his robe, and fought back more tears.

Light came in through the windows, cheery and bright. There had to be some way he could get to Mal.

Only two guards stood at the inside of the door now. He hid himself among the blankets.

He closed his eyes, leaned his face into a quilted cushion, and let the tears come hot and silent.

Chapter Thirteen

He slept rough. Agony-filled dreams haunted him every time he let go and tried to claim a deeper sleep.

Several times he thought he heard Mal crying out. But of course it was a dream. Mal would never cry out. Hated to ask for help. Yet Dare had heard Mal's heartbeats when they embraced, when they made love. His husband's life force was loose-woven, quick to wildness, the pulsings like suns and streams. To Dare, Mal never felt tied down or imposed upon. He was not afraid to laugh or cry.

Dare dug deeper into the covers despite the day's summer warmth, his body searching for Mal, trying to feel him against him. But there was nothing.

About an hour into his rest, he heard, dimly, the guards changing shifts. Many must not have had any sleep for more than a full day.

Dare's mind would not rest. It jammed him up with scenarios of the courtyard, the bodies, and his own head and Mal's, facing each other, on twin execution blocks. He turned and turned in the bed for what seemed like hours. It was useless. Maybe he had dozed a little.

He sat up and saw in the leaning afternoon light two less battle-weary and more polished guards at his door.

When they saw he was awake, one of the guards opened the door and gave orders to the servants.

Dare had slept—or not slept—with his hands manacled. His wrists ached. He gave it little thought. He had bigger troubles.

He got up and went to the window, looking out at the bright sky. He lowered his gaze to the ravaged courtyard below. Red blood puddles still glistened but the bodies were gone. He smelled the edge of smoke on the air.

Tears welled but he quickly staunched them.

It was strange for him to remember that not too long ago he had stared out this window dreaming of lands beyond, of adventure and wonder. But he'd never imagined this.

With practiced grace, servants came into the room, two bearing trays of food, two empty-handed, but immediately at his side. He knew the routine, but these were strangers. New servants. Anyone who had known him from his previous life had been killed this morning.

Dare knew his way round Darius's closet for he'd shared it all these years. If he was going to play the prince, he was going to do it with all the regal grandeur he had learned from being a prince's companion, servant and bed-warmer. And, for all of a couple of months, a prince's husband.

He chose from among the vast numbers of shirts, trousers and vests the colors that were richest, the materials that were the finest. Today he wore red trimmed in fine gold over a stark white shirt with gold ties, and sleek black trousers. The guard allowed his manacles to be taken off for dressing and eating his late lunch.

He felt as if he were back to his old routine at Shastan, before and during his secret visits to Prince Malory. That time the stakes concerned himself and possible war. This time the stakes were higher. The life of his love. He would give his own life to save him.

With his hair brushed to a shine, clothing impeccable, posture straight, he waited. He swept his gaze over the valley they had ridden through last night. Nothing had changed. It was all the same. And yet, everything was different.

Time passed and the sun began to set.

Finally, he heard a commotion outside of the guarded doors.

Andrus walked in. "You are summoned to court."

Wordless, Dare rose, chin high, and followed him into the corridor.

*

Two sculpted dragons crouched at the throne doors, looking ready to pounce.

Inside the throne room, things were different than Dare remembered. The throne had changed. The old throne had been dark, made of black polished wood. Now it was a marble monstrosity with purple silk cushions affixed to the back and the seat.

It was not something Dare thought the king would have chosen for himself. But with the new council and everything in upheaval for the months he'd been gone, Dare realized there must have been things going on that were more than just a mad king's whims.

In a shocking display of conceit, Lord Brandon sat in a casual pose upon that new throne. He had one foot stretched out, one hand draped over the chair arm. He wore a short purple cloak, lightweight for summer but trimmed with a thin line of white angora. Amethysts and rubies flashed at his throat and on his fingers.

Dare could not hold back his emotion of incredulity. Lord Brandon was not a king. This could not happen in front of the entire court. Not this fast.

As if reading his mind, Brandon motioned Dare close to him. The guards pushed Dare forward until he stood at the base of the throne looking up. Brandon did not ask him to kneel, or bow. Instead, he spoke in a soft voice laced with an arrogant timbre.

"The emergency council session ended less than an hour ago. Don't look shocked, Prince Darius." Brandon said the name with a slight hiss. "You are a prisoner of this kingdom, and I am the viceroy in charge now. As per the laws of Brookfall, it is my duty to oversee a fair and just trial for collusion culminating in regicide against the king of Brookfall. Until such time as a new king is crowned."

Of course as nephew and only living heir left to even make a claim for the throne, that new king would be Lord Brandon.

112

Dare now knew that had been Brandon's plan all along, but the meet at the border had given him the opportunity to hasten things along once he found out the real prince was dead.

The throne was placed intentionally high, designed to make anyone standing or kneeling before it feel small. Dare felt the muscles in his neck strain, still bruised from the king's own hands.

"I see," Dare said, keeping his voice low as well. "As viceroy, you have the power the grant lowly requests?"

Brandon's lips curved up, but he was not smiling. "I do."

"The king tried to kill me. I have the bruising to prove it. I will plead guilty to murder in self defense. You can do with me as you please. But I will only do this if you allow Mal to go."

"Self-defense killing is not an execution offense," said Brandon coldly. "What benefit do I have in accepting that plea simply to save you? And why would I accept it to save the enemy prince?"

Voice a whisper, Dare replied, "To save *you*."

"My life and actions are not in question here."

Dare thought hard. Softly, he said, "But I will take the fall for *your* crime. That is not good enough?"

Brandon leaned down until his chin was almost touching Dare's temple. "It would leave you alive, and still with your secret. Besides, you might blab." Brandon leaned back, smiling.

The court around them watched, but not all was silent. There were rustles of satins and ruffles, low murmurs from the sidelines, the sound of metal scraping metal each time a guard shifted his weight.

People were nervous. They knew Dare was their prince, but also part responsible for the king's death. They wanted to know more but none could hear what was transpiring. It was making them nervous, it seemed, that the council members up front were shifting their feet.

"I think you should promise me more before I even consider anything you say," Brandon said through his fake, impassive leer, the whites of his teeth showing.

He had all the power. But none of the heart.

Although there had not been much heart in this kingdom, Dare had never met someone of Brandon's like. This man was worse than any mad king. Or Prince Darius with his spoiled tastes and cringing paranoia. This man was still young, not more than forty years, lean and hungry, and smart. He had the handsome dark visage of all the royal family, and he looked quite natural sitting above everyone.

The ruthlessness with which he'd killed the king bespoke a smaller heart than his troubled uncle and cousin. If it even existed, truly what made up Brandon's heart must be in the shape of a blade.

"What would you have me promise?" asked Dare.

"Your confession might be nice, with an earnest request that as your cousin, I am the next rightful heir and you approve it."

Dare nodded. "Let Mal go. Like I said, I don't care what happens to me. If you save him, I will do all you tell me to do. Anything."

"But you already will."

"For Mal I will endure more. I will confess to regicide in self-defense. I will accept a guilty plea, and then I will recommend you as rightful heir."

"For his life. For your *lover*."

Dare closed his eyes tight, then opened them. "For my husband!"

"It is amusing to me that a servant would ever take that tone with any royal member of this household. And he cannot be your husband if you married under false pretenses. In fact, I myself can proceed to annul such a counterfeit marriage."

114

The council members were conferring among themselves to the right of the throne. Dare could not hear them. The guards were at attention, but far enough away that Dare's and Brandon's whispers would not be heard. Still, Dare was nervous. And talk of annulment made him angry. He clamped down on his fury.

"I have other ideas of what to do with you. I must say that having your cooperation makes everything easier. But I already have that, do I not? I already hold the life of Prince Malory in the palm of my hand."

"I know. And I have already said I will do anything to keep him alive. But I can make this ruse go even easier for you. I'm a good enough actor, as you've seen. No one has ever suspected I am not the real prince. I can play my part well in contrition. I can throw my support your way so that all will love and adore you. But there has to be a plan and promises."

Behind Dare, the court grew more restless. No one could overhear them. Yet. But Dare felt strange to be whispering all this in front of so much of an audience.

"Shouldn't we discussing all this away from the court? Have this negotiation in private?" Dare asked.

"Are you stupid? There is no negotiation happening."

Dare almost tripped backward. His mind reeled.

"Then I have nothing to lose by *not* cooperating with you." Dare's voice was flat and hard.

Lord Brandon leaned back, the strange smile still pasted on his face. He made a casual motion with his right hand and a guard came forward.

"Have Prince Darius escorted to the king's private meeting rooms."

"At once, Lord Viceroy."

*

Dare was losing ground quickly, but he almost felt as if he'd won something when he was taking from the court.

115

Soon, he sat with manacled hands in his lap while Lord Brandon paced the length of the long meeting table. The guards had been dismissed.

Dare kept his eyes on him, noting how Brandon's back was overly straight, one hand curled in a fist, the other loose, his fingers moving rapidly as if he were counting.

Brandon said, "You are an insipid little mimic, aren't you?"

Dare knew that question was not aimed for an answer.

"Tedious. You invite provocation," continued Brandon.

"You know my weaknesses," Dare said. "I'm offering them to you. All I care about is that Prince Malory goes free. It's easy enough to blame me. Say you were mistaken about Mal's confession, that the murder happened quickly, in a blur, and that you could not intervene in time. You can still save face. You can say you saw us both struggling with the king, but that I am the one who hit him with the tankard. You can even say you were trying to protect my honor by not jumping to the conclusion that I held the tankard, that I killed the king. It will look good for you."

"Lies never look good on any king who admits them."

"It would not be seen as a lie, but your confusion. All was a blur, but you now realize I held the tankard, not Mal."

Brandon looked thoughtful. "Continue."

Dare took a deep breath. "I will confess. I will uphold your claim to the throne as legitimate. How can it get better than that for you?"

"You will already do these things, or your beloved will die."

"He's already dead. You'll execute him anyway. But you can let him go. If I know he's gone away from here. If I know he's safe, then—then you can have anything from me."

Brandon turned and put his palms flat on the long table. "And if he tells the world of your secret and mine?"

"He won't."

"You can never know that," said Lord Brandon.

"He pledged to me to keep my secret to his death," said Dare. "With his very honor! He would never reveal it if he knew it would mean my death."

Brandon scowled. "Just words. I cannot know that for sure."

"If you keep me alive, he will never betray me. But if you kill me, he might. And I can't know what would happen afterward. I will confess to murder in self-defense. You can put me in the dungeon and leave me there."

"And where you could reveal the secret at any time. To the guards. To the dungeon-master."

"Men in dungeons claim their innocence every day. No one ever believes them." He thought of Stix, how he called his prisoners his children and seemed to think they could be transformed.

"He must fuck like the best whore in all the kingdoms for you to sacrifice so much." Brandon's mouth turned down. His lips pursed as if he'd eaten something bitter.

Dare took the insult in stride. "He has never done anything to deserve this. Only I have lied." He felt his throat swell up quite suddenly. "I have impersonated royalty for my own gain. I deserve this, but he doesn't."

For a long time, silence reigned.

Lord Brandon's mouth relaxed. He leaned back. His fingers played with the polished tabletop, drumming a non-rhythmic beat. The candles in the iron candelabrum at the center of the table flickered as if a breeze had found its way in through long halls and locked doors.

Without emotion, the words coming slowly, Brandon said, "These are my terms."

Chapter Fourteen

An hour passed before they were finished.

Brandon wanted a written confession from Dare, signed and dated. He wanted guarantees that once Mal was released, he would not change his mind and martyr himself for revenge. Or some misguided, last moment attempt to grab the throne.

Dare had never been greedy for power. As a servant, the mere idea of it was out of his hands. He did not envy kings. Most of Dare's life, the only prince he knew had been miserable. He enjoyed the luxuries. The education. The food. The wardrobe. But not the power.

He wrote out everything Brandon asked him to. He signed with a quill. He gave him all he wanted with an upright posture, an honest bearing, though there were some details that made him cringe.

Brandon appeared to be somewhat of a sadist. But unlike the dungeon-master Stix in Shastan, he made no apologies for his hardness, and his penchant to see more blood.

One of the terms Brandon insisted on was that it would look too easy if he simply let the enemy prince depart without some repercussions.

"A public flogging for Prince Malory."

"No!" Dare put down the quill.

"He has dishonored this kingdom. He is the enemy. If I show haste in my lenience, it will not play well."

Dare's breath shuddered in his lungs. Everything was about playing well. The theater of it all. Acting. Pretense.

Mal would fight all of it. He would not understand what Dare was doing. He might have accepted that Dare had played the part of prince to save his own life. They'd begun to fall in love at that point. Then Mal had used his own strengths to protect him. All for love.

But this, while also for love, would be harder for Mal to accept. Because Mal would never want to give up Dare. Not for any reason.

Dare said, "You can release him on good faith, for peace between the kingdoms. He does not need to be hurt any further."

"He does. And you will not only allow it, you will witness it."

Elbow on the table, Dare leaned his head into his palm, shaking it. "You choose to be heartless when you don't have to."

"I am a fair man. I am relenting to your requests. Does that not show you I am not thoroughly cruel?"

Dare did not deign to answer.

"It is good business," Brandon said. "That is all. If you think it is more than that, you are deluded."

Dare peered at him from across the table. "But you've already won. You don't need to take more and more!"

"In the eyes of the people, I am new. Untried. I need to show the firm hand."

"You enjoy it."

Brandon looked taken aback. "My dear boy. You are worth nothing. You are less than dirt to me. And you are a conspirator. You and the enemy prince, spreading for each other, you bending over him. For him! For all I know, you let Darius die so you could take his place and run wild. Of course I enjoy seeing you suffer. You are both a blight upon this realm."

Dare heard himself breathe in. Breathe out. He heard it like a wind in his ears, in his mind. A wind that wanted, badly, to create a storm.

He had already seen so much blood. He wanted an end to it. But more, he wanted Mal safe.

Voice low, he tried hard not to sound as broken as he felt. "The flogging will not be past a ten count. And you will let me tend him afterward."

"You do not get to set any terms!"

Dare said, "I *will* set them. For this. For this one thing."

Brandon's dark brows narrowed. "You will tend him. And then you will tell him that if he does anything at all to compromise my rule or this kingdom, your own life will be mine to command, to torture, to forfeit."

Dare could barely comprehend the words for the images that crossed his mind. Mal on the whipping post. Mal bared for all to see, whipped to the blood. It was awful. Second only to Mal's death.

Dare had gone through a whipping at the hands of Stix. It had been more painful than he could describe. But somehow this was worse. Watching the one you love hurt, humiliated, punished. And for nothing he had done wrong.

It was Dare's doing. All of it. Every choice he'd made from the day he'd been kidnapped led to this moment. He would save Mal. It was all he had left to give. And then when Mal was gone, his heart would break. But he would face that endurance test later.

*

Sent back to his rooms to wait until the hour before dusk, Dare paced. He could not sit. He could not eat. He could not think clearly.

Lord Brandon had forbidden him to be with Mal until after the flogging. The plan: Dare would be allowed to tend to Mal's wounds directly after the whipping. The next morning, Prince Malory would be banished from the kingdom of Brookfall, sent home under guard as a gesture of good will and peace.

No council member or courtier in either kingdom would argue that the Lord Viceroy was not a generous and forgiving man, intent on keeping war at bay and treating royal heirs—even murderous royal heirs—with honor and grace.

As the sun dipped lower and the light turned golden, Dare's stomach did flip after flip.

Mal would be forced to be readied now, his clothing ripped from him. His chains tightened. He would guess what was happening. He might wonder if he would die without a trial, and if Dare himself were already dead.

Dare forced himself to take deep breaths as he sat at the familiar seat at the window where he had always gazed out while growing up.

For a moment, he imagined Darius alive and well, sitting at the desk, bored and angry at homework he had no interest in, getting ready to order Dare to do his lessons for him. They both had been getting too old for tutors anymore. Adults, but they had a few more months of book learning to complete before their tutor moved on. Those months had been lost when the king had decided to declare war on Shastan.

Dare watched as a pole was erected in the courtyard, pounded into a hole in the ground and steadied with ropes and iron stakes. He had seen this before only a few times in his life. The king had been surly, but he did not normally whip men in public. That was what the dungeons were for.

Slowly, a crowd started to form. At first only a few onlookers. Townspeople. Farmers. Soon the crowd grew.

Dare knew the courtiers would be gathering on the flower and ivy-draped balconies which he could not see from his vantage. They would watch the proceedings apart from the ordinary people, keeping themselves high up, elevated from the masses. The wealthy did not like it if even a little blood spattered their fine clothing.

His front teeth bit hard on his lower lip as if pain might ease some of the tension. All it did was make him want to yell, hit a wall, a guard. Anything to stop this helplessness.

Behind him, Dare heard the door open. He turned.

Andrus stood tall in the doorframe wearing only the chest armor and not the full suit of metal. He wore a leather battle skirt and a black, short-sleeve shirt. His legs and arms were bare, showing off his power even more than if he'd come fully armored with sword in hand.

"The Lord Viceroy wishes you to accompany him to the courtyard."

Dare's insides heated with foreboding. His skin felt as if it were burning. One foot in front of the other. One step at a time. Shoulders back. Chin up.

Wordlessly, Dare followed the guard into the corridor.

*

Everything seemed shadowed with sparks flickering out the edges of Dare's vision. Sound was muffled. He smelled Lord Brandon before he saw him, the slickness of him as if he had freshly bathed in lavender-scented waters. He had indulged himself. Prepared for this moment of torture. This murderer, this nephew whom the rightful king had sent away. Maybe there was a reason for paranoia in this family. Maybe all the royal family did was hurt and betray each other.

"You will stand by my side during the entire event," Brandon ordered. "Your manacles will be fastened behind you."

"Hidden?"

A dark, elegant eyebrow rose. "For better security."

"So you still don't trust me," Dare said.

"Of course not."

"Perhaps you do not understand the value of the prince's life to me. We have a deal. I will not go back on it." Dare surprised himself when his voice came out firm and steady.

"Nothing is a sure deal."

When they moved through the open doors to the tops of the steps, the late daylight blinded Dare for a moment. He blinked away the sting and tried not to falter.

"You would think you were the one being led to the post," whispered Lord Brandon.

"I am."

Brandon let out a small, incomprehensible laugh. A combination of bitter and cruel.

They moved forward and down the wide, stone steps in a swish and swirl of fine leathers, imported satins, brocade, and lightweight summer cloaks.

For a moment Dare looked up, directly into the sun. For a moment, he thought it must all be a dream. Soon he would wake in Mal's arms shaking but alive. Safe.

Instead, when he looked straight ahead, his eyes clearing from the leftover light flashes on his retinas, he saw Mal, bloody and stumbling and in chains, being forced through the parting crowd. But for a loincloth, he was completely naked. The bruising on his body showed, along with gashes that had barely scabbed over on his knee and his chest. It was hard at first to see the prince behind all that blood and bruising and dirt. But there was no mistaking that long, lean-muscled body and, even chained, the feline grace and proud temperament of Malory, the Crown Prince of the Kingdom of Shastan, outshone the crowd.

Dare's heart felt as if it was coming out of his chest. He wanted to scream out to the bloodthirsty crowd. Cry. Beg for lenience. He could do nothing if he wanted Mal to go free.

His back itched with sweat. Lord Brandon, beside him, looked cool as winter. Clean as a new day. Divine and justified.

It was so wrong.

For a moment, Mal looked up and around him, through tangled spirals of golden curls. Dare knew that gaze was searching for him.

When their eyes met his heart quaked as if cleaved in half. Everything came starkly into focus. The pink-edged, dusk-trenched sky. The blackbirds wheeling high overhead. The hastily mopped cobblestones where blood had already been spilled in the dark hours of the morning.

Mal's resplendent majesty, a charismatic glow, could not be dampened even by dirt or blood.

Even the nervous crowd had quieted. For they, too, could see that this was no common criminal or enemy, but a man who would one day be a king and who held his head high and proud despite the obvious exhaustion of his body.

Mal was too far away for Dare to see all that might be contained in his eyes. But he knew. Those tawny depths would be filled with worry over Dare's fate, determined not to let Dare down.

Now, even more so, Dare knew he was doing the right thing by making this deal with Lord Brandon.

Mal did not fight the guards who pushed him toward the whipping post. The chains on his wrists looked too tight, the skin about them red and blistered.

Mal's ankles were free, but there was a line of bright pink encircling each that showed the crowd his bindings at his feet overnight had been cruel. The knife cuts across his fine chest and on his upper arm were also slightly swollen and pink, but they were not festering with life-threatening liquids. Luckily, they looked dry, though untreated.

Dare's chest shivered as he watched the guards push Mal face-first to the post and kick his legs apart.

Wide, long stakes had been pounded into the stony ground and the guards attached chains to them and then to Mal's ankles. Another guard gagged him with a black cloth, then raised Mal's shackled hands over his head and attached a chain through the manacles and around the post, pulling as tightly as he could.

Mal's forehead pressed the wooden post. His hair, which was long and curly at the nape, was grabbed and twisted up and over the gag's knot with a painful tug by the same guard who'd chained his arms. A metal comb fixed it in place. Now his whole back was exposed.

The dungeon-master strode through the crowd, ready to do the whippings himself. At that moment, Lord Brandon stepped away from Dare's side and moved forward, already dispensing with his cloak and folding his untied sleeves up past his elbows.

He turned toward the crowd. "This traitor and conspirator against the king of Brookfall is deserving of the lash. And more. I'm sure you will all agree. But new knowledge has come to us that he is, in fact, not the actual murderer. The king's own son, Prince Darius of Brookfall, has confessed to the crime of patricide and regicide. He claims self-defense. His own trial on that matter will commence in a few days."

The crowd went wild, shouting and hollering, beating their fists into the air.

Lord Brandon held up his hand for silence. "For now, Prince Malory of Shastan, for your part in colluding with the prince of Brookfall, your punishment shall be fifty lashes."

Dare jerked in shock. That had *not* been their deal. He started to move forward but was held back in a firm grip by Andrus.

"However, there is still the matter of a peace treaty to be handled, and in good faith I myself, as Viceroy to Brookfall, have amended that punishment to twenty lashes."

The crowd booed.

"He will be banished from this kingdom forever and sent back to his home in disgrace and dishonor. And the true murderer, Prince Darius, will be brought to justice for this crime before you all. This is my word and is not to be contested."

There were shouts and a few murmurs, but the crowd settled after a few moments, respecting their new viceroy's word.

Dare watched Mal's head shake. Mal pulled at his bonds to no effect, trying to make sounds against his gag.

Dare wanted to look away. He couldn't look away. Later, they would speak and he would make Mal understand why he had made his confession.

The crowd stood back, held in place by palace guards. For now, there was nothing he could do. Absolutely nothing.

Dare glanced over Mal's head to see more people gathering. In that moment, he saw someone he knew and froze. A girl his own age. The daughter of one of the kitchen servants. Her name was River.

Dare had known her growing up. She was cloaked, standing at the back of the crowd unnoticed. But her dark eyes met his and Dare grew suddenly afraid she would be caught and summarily butchered.

Everyone he saw in the castle these past two days had been new. In the early hours of the morning when he'd arrived, there had been so many bodies. It had not occurred to him that some of the servants who might know him had escaped. He felt stupid not to think of it. That there might be people still about who would recognize him and keep silent. Hidden.

River's life was in danger. She had to know it. Then why was she here? Did she hate him now? Did she come to see his husband flogged and revel in the just punishments of two colluding princes?

More people pushed and shoved to the front of the crowd, obscuring River. Dare could do nothing for her and hoped she would be all right.

Lord Brandon approached the dungeon-master, someone Dare had only seen a couple times in his life who typically stood with the council members at the king's side during formal trials. Trials were rare in Brookfall, for the king himself usually judged and passed sentence on the spot. Either the dungeon-master or the executioner saw the sentences to their fruition.

The dungeon-master handed Brandon the whip, almost reluctant to let go of the leather-braided handle studded with silver stars. The dungeon-master said nothing and did not spare one glance for Dare.

Dare winced as he saw Brandon raise the whip, testing its weight. His hands curved into tight fists, his fingernails digging into his palms.

Brandon walked closer to where Mal, shoulders tense, feet awkwardly spread, was chained. He walked up to Mal's back and leaned in, saying something low into his ear.

Mal's only reaction was to stand up straighter and toss his head.

The viceroy stepped back. His hand rose. Came back. The end of the whip sang through the air and ended with a thwack.

Dare jumped. Andrus's hand tightened on his arm.

Dare tasted bile in the back of his throat when he saw the first red weal on Mal's back turn crimson and fill with blood.

When Dare had been whipped in the Shastan dungeon it had been ten lashes to the blood. He remembered it as if it had happened yesterday. His back itched whenever he thought of it, that acrid, metallic pain that swept into his brain and left its white ash behind.

Ten lashes had been unbearable. But he'd felt that Stix had held back, had not used full force. His wounds had healed quickly and well with Mal's gentle touch and the healing salves he and the healers used on him twice a day. Mal would be getting twenty lashes and leaving in the morning. He'd be in bad shape to travel.

The second strike came, a little lower. Dare jumped again. Mal's body looked stretched taut, the muscles like rocks under his skin, twitching.

At the third strike, Dare let out a small groan.

The crown was yelling for blood. Urging Brandon on.

Brandon stood tall, perfectly posed, unyielding. No blood spatter, yet, on his white shirt and fine trousers.

Strike four and five left heavier marks on Mal's lower back. Mal's head was bent now, forehead pressed hard to the post.

It appeared he barely felt strikes five through seven. But Dare felt each and every one, his body startling with each crack of the whip. His heart throbbing with needle-like stabs of pain.

By the tenth, tears burned down Dare's cheeks. Once the strikes entered the teens, Mal's body was slumped. No longer fighting the contact of whip against skin. Maybe he was unconscious by now. His back was striped, the blood shining against the skin like rubies.

Brandon's shirt had little speckles of blood now; they showed when he drew back the whip to strike again.

The crowd grew louder around them, but Dare heard it only as an irritating buzzing. His sole focus was on Mal and how soon he could have him in his arms to wipe away the blood, soothe his pain, and promise now and forever that no more harm would ever come to him.

He felt sick but held it in. For Mal he needed to be strong as the last three strikes left their damage on Mal's beautiful body.

When Lord Brandon was finished, he handed the bloodied whip to a servant and turned away, fiddling with his cuffs as if he did this every day and it was no big drama.

The crowd shouted ugly words at the prince.

"Scourge of Shastan."

"Prince Whore."

"Cocksucker."

"Pig fucker."

The words were the worst of the gutter language from the streets. Darius had perfected them all, and made Dare learn them with him. So they weren't any words he hadn't heard, but they were the most vile that could be said.

As three guards began to undo the chains on Malory's slumped body, Dare started to walk forward.

Brandon came toward him and said, "No."

Dare looked up at him, trying not to see the tiny splatters of blood on his sleeves and shirt shoulder.

"You can't run to him in front of all these people," Brandon said in his ear as he passed by. "Come with me."

Andrus pushed Dare to turn and follow Brandon into the castle entrance. Over his shoulder, he saw Mal slumped in the hold of two guards who dragged him in the opposite direction toward the high walls of the dungeon set apart from the castle. Mal's bare feet scraped along the stones.

Dare's face itched where drying tears tracked his cheeks.

Lord Brandon walked gracefully ahead of him, confident and unconcerned.

Dare had never understood cruelty in any form. He had abided Darius's bullying and odd predilections only because he knew Darius suffered from disproportionate fear and a melancholia that manifested as unchecked anger. Dare never approved of it, or liked it.

Lord Brandon had other qualities that seemed worse, an odd detachment that did not derive from anger, but more from showmanship. He wanted to be the focus. He wanted to be in charge. And he didn't care who he destroyed to attain that.

Dare stumbled after him, moving fast to keep up. Andrus stayed beside him with his hand on his arm the entire way to the king's office.

Once they were away from prying ears, with only Andrus at his side, Dare said, "I want to be taken to him now. As we agreed."

"Yes. Yes." Brandon waved his hand as if he could not be bothered. "Did you think I would allow the people to see you have any further contact with him? You are that stupid!" He glanced at Andrus, who stood unmoving by the door, a silent support, and added, as though for Andrus's benefit, "Silly servant boy! You could never have ruled. You would be a terrible king."

While Brandon sorted through papers and pretended to be officious and busy, Dare waited. His pulse pounded. All he could think was that right now Mal was probably thrown into a filthy cage and left on his own to wake in shock and pain.

Finally, Brandon looked up. He said to Andrus, "As soon as the crowd has dispersed, you will cloak him. Then you will take him to Prince Malory. Lock them in together, I don't care. The prince will be gone by morning and we can get on with more important matters here in the realm, including the trial of Prince Darius."

Andrus bowed. "Yes, Viceroy."

Chapter Fifteen

It was humid in the passages that led underground, and dark dust floated on dim light from the ancient oil lamps on the walls. Cobwebs drifted from the ceiling on dank air.

Andrus followed behind Dare as two burly dungeon guards led them through the passageways.

One guard mumbled to the other, "It's not every day we get two princes gracing our presence."

The other laughed. Andrus, wisely, said nothing.

They came around a curve in the hall, and the taller guard took a key from beneath his cloak. There was a screech of metal on metal, then the yowl of old hinges as the barred door swung open.

Dare came alongside the guard to peer into the shadowy cell. He saw Mal lying on his stomach on a pallet that was mostly string and wadded cloth. The bare, stone floor was blackened from time and filth.

Dare made a quick step forward, but Andrus held him back. "Hold it!"

"I am allowed to go in."

"I know," Andrus said quietly.

He took a key from his own pocket and undid the manacles on Dare's wrists. Then he handed him the package Dare had demanded, a satchel of healing salves and clean cloths and bandages, and assorted tinctures for pain and infection to be taken by mouth. He also handed him a skin of fresh water.

"Don't let him sleep on his back tonight."

"I know." Dare looked up at Andrus, seeing him as a person in that moment. "Thank you."

Andrus let out a huff of air. "I'll be here until dawn when you are to be escorted back to the castle."

Dare stepped into the room.

*

Mal was awake. One dull eye stared at him as Dare knelt by his side.

Dare reached out to Mal's bare shoulder. Mal still wore only the loincloth, His back was exposed, a map of terror, intersections, and scarlet roads that crisscrossed over muscle, rib, spine.

Mal cringed at the touch.

"It's all right. I have oils to tend your wounds."

"You have nothing," Mal said, voice rough as sand. He coughed and then moaned in pain as the movement pulled at the wounds on his back.

"I know. It is all my fault."

"I didn't mean it like that."

"It's all right. I missed you. They let me come see you. Finally! I'm here to help you."

"You have nothing because you'll be dead in days. Why did they let you come see me? Why did you confess? Dare?" Mal's voice broke. "Why?"

"And hello to you, too," Dare replied quietly.

"I missed you, too," Mal said through gritted teeth.

Gently, Dare said, "This isn't your plan anymore. It's mine. I'm going to make sure you're safe. For good."

"Oh, fuck," Mal said, as he tried to move again. "There will be no more safety. Whether I die here now, or go back to Shastan without you. My own father the king will declare war himself. So many will die. But not you, Dare. I had it figured that you would be alive even if incarcerated."

"Listen to yourself. It's all right for you to plan to save me but not for me to do it in return?"

Silence. Then, "No. It's not all right."

Dare took a deep breath. "I love you. How can I not do what I did?"

"Just shut up."

132

"Mal—"

"If you keep talking like that," said Mal, "I'll weep and then I won't stop."

Dare ran his hand through Mal's soft, knotted curls. "Let me see what I can do for your back. You're going to have to ride tomorrow."

Mal only groaned.

It was fairly bad, the skin split and reddening, but Mal was so lean that many of the cuts were not deep, having been thwarted by hard, lean muscle. A few were problematic, but he had more physical strength than he showed when fully dressed. Those muscles had helped protect him.

Slowly, methodically, Dare cleaned all the wounds, then rubbed salve into the cuts and onto the bruises and burns. He took long, torn pieces of linen and wrapped Mal's upper body tightly.

"These dressings will have to be changed tomorrow," Dare said. "And more salve applied. I hope there will be someone to help you." His voice broke. He took more deep breaths to control himself.

Mal said, "We'll have matching scars."

Dare leaned away when he was finished, back against the wall, and helped Mal lift himself into a sitting position so he could drink some water. It was summer, so the dungeon did not get too cold at night.

Dare placed his cloak, balled up, into his lap like a cushion. Then he brought Mal's upper body half onto his thighs. Mal lay partially on his side, one knee bent.

"I don't want to leave you behind." Mal sighed.

Dare replied, "Understand this. I don't want to watch your head become detached from your body."

In a dejected voice, Mal said, "Understood. But what about you? The trial will be a sham, of course. They'll find you guilty even though you're not."

"I have a deal. I will live."

"So that bastard says. He killed the king. Don't trust him, Dare."

"Believe me, I don't."

Dare stroked Mal's hair again. After a while, he asked, "I know you can't move much, but how are the cuts on your knee and chest?"

"They bled a lot, but they're not deep. They'll heal," came the muffled response.

Dare held him tighter to his chest, pushing the hair away from Mal's forehead. He hoped Mal dozed, but by his still shallow breathing, suspected he was in too much pain to do anything but lie quietly and suffer.

Out of the silence, Mal's voice drew softly about them. "You came into my kingdom quite suddenly, as if you were lifted from one of my innermost private dreams."

"Yes, and then ruined your life." Dare let his fingers go still in Mal's hair, as if they were now part of the tangles.

"No. You didn't ruin it. All the things happening were in play regardless of you or me. You know that."

"I didn't know. I was only a servant. I did as I was told, remember?" Dare's voice was soft.

"I didn't know that when I saw you. You looked every inch a prince."

Dare let out a sound of disbelief.

"I know all this hasn't been easy for you, so much change," Mal said.

"No. That's not true."

"But it's hard—"

"No. It's the easiest thing I've ever done," said Dare, never so certain of anything in his life. "To fall in love with you. All this death and I'm still so happy I found you. I feel guilty for it sometimes. But it's easy. The easiest thing I've ever done."

"Me, too."

Dare's heart swelled. "The hardest thing about it is walking around all the time feeling like my chest is ripped

134

open and my heart is exposed for all to see, beating in the air. Raw. Vulnerable. Beating just for you. It's ecstasy and agony. But this?" He gestured around them at the filthy straw, the stained rock walls of the dungeon. "This is easy. Because of you. Because I know you'll live now. And I will live. And maybe, one day, we'll meet again."

Mal's breath grew hitched. He stayed quiet, but his shoulders had a tremble in them that Dare knew meant he was trying to keep himself emotionally together, in control.

Dare had not lied. It was easy. He'd always lived for others, at their whims, obeying commands, simple or insane. He was used to it. Used to doing demoralizing things like being a human footstool, used to improper respect, or no respect at all.

Horrible things had happened, but then he'd met Mal. For those moments of joy they had together, he felt lucky. He was the luckiest man alive.

He could weather anything as long as he knew Mal lived.

His eyes passed over the long legs, bare against the hard stone. The loincloth ended just where the lean thighs met the curve of buttocks. The golden skin of Mal's legs was mostly unblemished. The tops of his ass peeked out from the upper gathering of the cloth below his waist, showing two perfect dimples on either side of his spine. Mal's ribs showed above his waist where the bandages began. He had such a perfect body, so hard and slippery, and sweet to hold.

Even through all this suffering, Dare felt himself warm to it, felt pleasure in seeing his lover, in holding his lover, course through his veins. He never wanted this feeling to end.

The long hours of the night passed. But they were still too short. They had too little time together.

Dare let his head bow low in his tiredness, until his face was buried in Mal's curls. He held him gently, one hand snaked beneath Mal on Mal's bare skin above the bandages covering his chest, one hand on his bare shoulder. Mal's own fingers gripped tightly at Dare's thigh.

It was just the two of them, in shadow-painted astonishment at such peace, such perfection. Gone was the dungeon and the outside world. Only they remained, and their love. A breath of newness, of gold. A wish fulfilled on all levels.

When pre-dawn turned the shadows a more rosy brown, and more guards could be heard shuffling in the hall, Mal moved his body a bit and tried to sit up.

Dare helped him. Gave him more water.

Then Mal said, as they heard a jingling of keys heading their way, "I will get you back. No matter what I have to do. I'll come for you."

Dare leaned forward. Their lips met. And all the beauty of the world Dare could not see right now flowed in his veins like a gift waiting for him to find.

A key scraped against the cell's lock. Their time together was up.

Chapter Sixteen

Dare didn't care about the guards at his door. He didn't care about pulling his clothes off in front of them, and tossing them to the floor for the servants to gather.

Without a word, Dare crawled into the sweet-scented, freshly made bed of the dead Prince Darius, sobbed once, then fell to sleep.

For the second time in two days he was allowed to sleep until the sun was high in the sky. This time, when he woke, it wasn't to the sounds of servants coming into the room, or guards giving noisy orders at the door.

It was to the sight of one man.

He stood in a wide ray of light coming through Dare's favorite window. Immaculate in appearance, dark head bowed, hands clasped loosely in front of his body, Lord Brandon, the new viceroy of Brookfall, watched Dare with a keen, dark eye.

This new day he wore a clean white shirt--not blood-spattered--and a gold brocade waistcoat. His black trousers ended in knee-high black leather boots.

Dare sat up, his hair in his eyes, the thin cover falling from his naked chest.

"Did Prince Malory get off all right?"

"He is gone."

"Then what are you—? What is it?"

Lord Brandon tilted his head. His eyes held no expression. "Oh, you're asking me why I am here?"

Dare nodded.

"I own you now."

Dare's brows rose. "But is my trial—"

"Yes, your trial is being planned for the day after tomorrow. That is the show to be played before the court."

Dare blinked. Of course it was a show. It was all lies. Just like everything in his life had been from the moment he'd been forced to play the prince when he and Darius were no more than twelve.

Brandon had a look in his eye like cold gusts. "Get up," he said.

Dare did not, at first, understand the command.

"Get up! I don't want to have to repeat myself again."

Dare moved his legs under the coverlet and scooted to the edge of the bed. His body was sore. His neck ached from still unhealed bruises. He reached for the robe a servant had laid across the foot of the bed.

"Leave it," Brandon said.

Dare glanced up at him again, his hand frozen in mid-air.

"Stand before me," Brandon commanded.

At the side of the bed, Dare sat naked with not even a jewel left to adorn his body and only his dead mother's thin silver bangle hugging his wrist, which he'd worn since he was a child. A part of him didn't care that he was so exposed. But still he hesitated.

Brandon lifted his hand with a casual flip. "Guard!"

Movement at the door, a silvery shift of light. Andrus stepped forward.

Dare scooted off the bed, letting the covers fall. "I'm standing, all right?"

The air was warm. His nude body did not chill or flush. It had no reaction as he obeyed the order of Lord Brandon. But deep inside, a fever of worry began.

The predilections of Darius had been demoralizing. The king had looked the other way. Was the nephew no different? Would he be a footstool for Brookfall's new viceroy to order about as he saw fit?

Dare forced himself to breathe shallow, to not sway, to keep his hands at his sides and not try to hide himself in shyness at the way Brandon's eyes gazed over his body. Up. Down. Back up.

"You do not deserve these rooms."

Dare should have looked down, bowed his head in respect to royalty. Instead, he continued his steady gaze at Lord Brandon's face.

"You do not deserve fine food or clothing," Brandon continued. "You should have been in the dungeon from the start. With nothing. Chained to a wall until the vermin ate you alive."

Dare's heart stopped, then started again.

"You should never have been seen in your lifetime. By anyone." Brandon's lips curved in a sideways 'S'. "A mere servant." As he said the last word, he spit. The liquid flew at Dare's chest, a warm spray.

It was strange the way Dare's mind reacted. He did not recoil. He did not feel any sting of tears. For fifteen years he'd built a sort of invisible armor against demeaning words from his supposed "betters". When he heard such words he felt himself grow apart from them, as if he lived in another world right alongside this one, and nothing really touched his heart. He didn't hate. And pathetic, insecure, nervous Darius was like a brother to him. But he didn't love, either. Not until he'd met Mal.

Mal was now safe, heading on horseback somewhere on the road to the border. Mal could occupy that other world again. And he would be all right no matter what. Both of them would be all right.

It occurred to Dare that Andrus had heard these comments. It was quite apparent now to Dare, if he hadn't been entirely sure before, that Andrus knew his true identity. But had he been in on the assassination of a king? Was he brought into the inner circle and promised rewards if he kept the secret?

"Do you have anything to say to that?" Brandon asked.

"No." Dare did not use the honorific *sire* or *lord* or *viceroy.*

Brandon showed a small flinch in the muscles along the left side of his neck.

"I came in here because I wanted to see what all the fuss was about. Princes having you live with them. Princes having you as bedmates. Your body is young and toned, of course. I'm sure most men would gleefully bend you over."

The beginnings of a flush heated Dare's cheeks but he was glad to note his veins did not burn in embarrassment or anger.

"You have a pretty pink-tipped cock. An asset fit for a whore. Which is, of course, what you are, and what you have always been."

Dare bit on the inside of his lower lip, but not hard enough to taste salt.

"A whore is what you are. And I own you now. Now do you understand?"

Dare let out a slow breath. "No."

"No?"

"Unless it means you're going to fuck me." Had those words come from his mouth? He had not even thought to hold them back until they were out.

"Why would I sully myself on you?" Brandon replied, turning his head.

Dare kept his muscles relaxed, though something deep inside him tensed.

Brandon was unpredictable. He'd let Dare tend to Mal's wounds in the dungeon cell, but he'd killed dozens of innocent servants and anyone else who'd known Dare growing up, including courtiers. They'd been executed as colluding traitors. None of them got a trial. But none of them were princes.

What drove Brandon was ambition at his own whim. He could change his mind in a heartbeat if it suited him. They had a deal, but Dare could not rely on any fact that Brandon

140

would keep his word about anything. Even now, he wondered if Mal really had been let go, though Brandon had announced it to the crowd.

Maybe, just maybe, Brandon truly did not wish for war and thought the gesture of sending the enemy prince back to his kingdom alive would keep the peace.

No, Dare had to believe Mal was safe. That Brandon had kept his word on that deal. Mal would be unhappy that Dare was left behind, but he would be safe and free.

Brandon interrupted his thoughts. "But then again, the guards might enjoy sullying themselves on you and I would not object."

Dare lifted his chin. The tension deep inside him grew.

"I would see your face covered with their emissions and not object."

Dare's thoughts went backward in a sort of white fury of memory. Darius had spoken this way to him often. Told him he was worthless. Less than a pet to him. His very own flesh and blood footstool.

Darius had enjoyed Dare's favors in bed, ordered and obeyed, and told him he sucked cock like a whore. That he was little better than a whore. Dare took it in stride, knowing Darius's mind, like that of a child, had festered from within with something he could not name.

Lord Brandon festered. But he had more power, and less fear than Darius. He showed no signs of excessive paranoia or tantrums or self-hatred. So far. Only ambition. And a sadistic streak that possibly even Stix, the dungeon-master of Shastan, could not match.

Like Darius, but not like Darius. As if Darius the boy had grown into a man overnight and become a self-assured monster, unafraid, a master at a game combining chess and torture.

They would have been cousins, Darius and Brandon. They would have been twenty-one years apart in age, but mirrors to each other on a stage of thrones and the ruling class.

"You should be paraded through the castle and along the paths and through the outlying towns naked in chains."

For the first time since waking to see Lord Brandon standing over him watching him sleep, Dare glanced away. Toward the archway. Toward Andrus who stood with a stoic expression, body blocking the center of the closed door.

This was the only guard whose name he'd gotten to know. Andrus had not been cruel to him. Andrus was not faceless. But was he in on all of it? Would he, in fact, rape Dare if ordered to do so?

Andrus's body language and eyes gave nothing away.

Dare turned back to Brandon, swallowing hard. If he cooperated, maybe it would never come to that. "I will do anything you say. You are right. You own me now."

"In two days we will have your trial. I need to get to know you better."

Confusion now. "Why?"

"There is a lot to plan for. I want to make sure you understand these plans implicitly, with no mistakes."

Do not trust him, Mal had said. And Dare didn't. But he had no choice but to comply.

"I said I will do what you say," Dare repeated, voice clipped.

Brandon turned to Andrus. "Get the servants in here. Get him dressed. Then take him to my chambers."

Andrus bowed. "Yes, Viceroy." He turned to open the door to the hall.

Dare stood naked, unmoving.

"Make it quick!" Brandon said, then strode toward the doorway and left the room.

Chapter Seventeen

Dare stood, fully clothed now, in the king's chambers.

Lord Viceroy Brandon poured water into two silver chalices from a blue ceramic pitcher.

"This water," he said, "is from the Moonmist springs of the Aliothe Mountains."

"It sounds very expensive," Dare replied.

He had a chain around one wrist fastened to a metal link embedded into the floor. Dare wondered if it had always been there. Or if Lord Brandon had had it fashioned overnight.

The length of the chain gave him the freedom to sit or stand, but not to move around more than a single step in any direction.

"It is. The purest form of liquid one can imbibe." Brandon walked over to Dare, offering him one of the chalices. "Would you care to try?"

Dare took the chalice in his unchained hand. He did not immediately drink. He merely watched as Brandon took his own chalice to an over-stuffed chair and sat facing him.

Dare looked away. He had never been in the king's chambers before. He and Darius had never been allowed inside. They were larger than Darius's quarters, with open doors leading to atriums and verandas. There were closed doors that led to mystery, perhaps clothing closets, or water closets, or bathing rooms. Or rooms of torture. Who could know?

One double doorway opened to a room with a huge bed on a raised dais. The covers on the bed were blood-red and purple. It had few pillows, and the rest of the decor looked sparse in that room, hardly used, the walls beige, the windows plain with undecorated frames.

In the main room there was more to see. Too much. Parchment-covered desks, plush chairs, a long table with trays of drink and food. The wood of all the furniture looked dark and old, the bases or legs intricately cared with dragons, or other monsters of lore. The marble floor was covered with ornate rugs in black, maroon or gold colorings.

Brandon drank deeply. Relaxed. And seemed to patiently wait until Dare had finished gazing about the rooms.

"Drink. It retains a taste of coldness I think you will like," Brandon said, once Dare's gaze returned to him.

Dare brought the chalice to his lips. The water was pure and cool, tasting faintly of rain on leaves. There was a distant sweetness to it, reminding him of Mal's fresh-from-the-bath skin when they had spent long nights for weeks on end after their wedding getting to know each other's bodies, inch by inch, over and over again.

After Dare swallowed he looked across the room at Brandon, who regarded him with a quirked eyebrow.

"Tell me," Brandon said. "Everything. From the beginning. What happened to Prince Darius? What was your part?"

Mal was the only one who knew Dare's full story. Now this stranger, this hollow man wanted to know everything. The story was not pretty. It still gave Dare nightmares.

"Leave nothing out," Brandon further instructed.

Dare closed his eyes and began at the point where the prince's party, with Dare impersonating the prince for safety's sake, disembarked on their journey to the Royal Chalet.

"No, go further back. I want to know who your mother was. Your father. How did you come to be in Prince Darius's company as his chattel, his boy?"

"I only know my mother's name. Gracie. I know nothing more. Only that when she died I was brought to live with the prince as his companion and personal servant."

"How did you get along?"

144

"All right, at first," said Dare, his mind going back to that confusing, yet more innocent time. "Not so much later when his tempers increased, when he refused to leave his rooms for weeks at a time."

Brandon continued to ask questions. Dare answered. He had no reason to hide anything from Brandon. It would all be over in two days anyway. If Brandon kept his word, Dare would be thrown in the dungeon for life.

He took a deep breath, and plunged into the details of his mercurial life with Darius. When he got to the part where Darius died in his arms, his voice croaked a bit.

"But of course you were glad he died," Brandon said. "You could take over. And all his supposed cruelties to you would never happen again."

Dare blinked. "I was not glad."

Brandon smirked in disbelief.

"It was horrible. I never thought about being free from him, only one day that he might be happy and finally stop tormenting me."

"Yet you continued your ruse as the prince."

"The Shastan guards mis-identified me. I thought they'd kill me if they knew the truth. I went along with them to stay alive. I didn't intend to keep impersonating the prince forever. And certainly not this long."

"But you did. And you still are."

Dare bowed his head. "I can't undo what I have done. I've given myself over to you now. I only ever hoped to save lives."

"Yet your crazy actions have caused more death than these two countries have seen in decades."

Dare's body reacted, flushing, then chilling all over. It was as if Brandon had stabbed him with those words. His throat thickened with the onslaught of his own conscience. It had all started with the king sending his son away. Nothing of Dare's own doing. He'd fallen into pit after pit until all he could think about was his next breath, surviving.

"No one has that kind of foresight," Dare said. "I only wanted to live."

"Yes. And there is no crime in that, is there? It can be said that I am in the same boat with you. The difference is, I have royal blood. I am born to it. You are a servant. You are nothing. That you might be so bold as to keep up this pretense is disgusting. An abomination."

Dare gulped in air. The chalice in his hand tilted. He gripped it harder. Bore down on the outrage and hurt that shuddered through him.

"We were mirrors to each other, but opposites, Darius and I," Dare said. "I never pretended otherwise with him. He knew it. He called me his Footstool."

"And that is your place in the world. Don't ever forget it." Brandon's eyebrows came together creating a crease in his otherwise smooth visage. He could have been a handsome man if he'd been infused with a soul.

Dare continued to glare.

"I'll have many more questions over the next couple of days. You will stay in these rooms, chained, where I can find you, where I can see you at all times. Where I can have total control over you."

Brandon nodded toward Dare's shaking hand that held the chalice. "Drink up. When your trial comes, I hope never to see you again."

He stood and left the room with a small bounce to his step, as if he had not just said the ugliest of words to another human being.

*

Dare sat on the stone floor with his knees bent, the water chalice at his side. He leaned against the wall and waited.

When Brandon returned hours later, he said, with preamble and barely a glance in Dare's direction, "Tell me about Prince Malory."

He tossed off his outerwear and his waistcoat. In his white shirt, which he'd unlaced to his breastbone, he walked to the table and poured himself some water.

Dare's water was drained. Brandon had been gone for at least two hours and Dare had been thirsty and drank his portion dry.

Without looking at him, Brandon said, "Stand in my presence, servant. And answer my question."

Dare's chain rattled as he scrambled to get up. His elbow bumped the wall.

"Wh—what about him?" Dare asked.

Turning a little too quickly, Brandon looked angry. As if his afternoon had not gone well. "Does he fuck like a whore, too?"

Dare took a deep breath. "He's an honorable man. Born to rule."

"That's not answering my question! And if you're insolent with me again, I'll have the guards come in—" He did not finish.

Dare knew what he meant.

"He thought I was the real prince. I'd been sick and he came to see me in the healer's quarter. He had been forbidden by his father to do so."

"So his father and he do not get along?"

"What father doesn't argue with his son? But they do get along." Dare wondered if Brandon thought he might interrogate Dare for Mal's weaknesses. But in Dare's mind, Mal didn't have any weaknesses. "Mal is decisive and strong and fair. He'll make a great king one day."

Brandon smiled but it did not look like he was happy. Just cruelly satisfied.

Dare nearly balked. Had he said too much? He didn't want to talk about Mal anymore.

147

"So he's as spoiled as Darius was," Brandon concluded.

Dare had thought that at his very first meeting with Prince Malory. He'd been wrong. "No."

"Every time you lie to me, it's a truth coming out."

Dare frowned. That made no sense.

"So why did you two come together? Did he rape you and you liked it?"

Dare did not answer. Brandon lacked empathy. He'd killed innocent people. He'd killed the king. He was a criminal mind of the worst persuasion. Dare could not allow himself to be surprised at these foul questions.

"Was my question too sensitive for you?"

Dare stared at the floor. He was unsure how to answer.

"Why would you be too sensitive to answer me," Brandon asked. "All you have done your whole life is kowtow to princes and pretend to be one."

Brandon walked over to Dare and took his chin into the palm of his hand, thrusting his head up. "You are mine now. You will do as I say. That is our deal."

Throat dry, Dare nodded.

"Then answer the questions!"

"H-he didn't rape me." Dare's voice came out low.

Still holding his chin, Brandon said, "He seduced you, then."

Dare did not know what to say. The hand on his chin tightened.

"Answer!"

"We—we fell in love."

"While you were still a hostage?"

"Yes."

The hand came away from Dare's jaw. "Interesting. A power play. Coercion. So much to work with."

"There was no coercion."

Brandon raised the same hand that had just held Dare's chin and smacked him. It was so sudden, Dare had no time to react. The pain came a moment later, splintering in needle flares on the skin of his cheek and in his jaw.

Dare looked up through blurred eyes.

Brandon's face was very close to his. Dare could smell the wine on his breath. He could see the flecks of green in his cold brown eyes.

"These are things you will say in court, of course. The part about you being a hostage and fucking the enemy prince will be played as coercion. It will make me look better when I give you leniency and spare your life."

It was all lies. There had been so many lies since Darius died. But the one thing that was not a lie was his love for Mal.

A shaking began deep inside him. He had made an agreement to save Mal's life. But could he say these lies—the ones about Mal—in front of the entire court of Brookfall?

The light through the balcony windows was dimming. The king's rooms faced the east, so the only sunset he could see was a purple sky speckled with two early stars.

Brandon made a plate of food at the table, then brought it, wordlessly, to Dare.

He unhooked Dare's chain and allowed him to relieve himself in the water closet, and to wash his hands and face. Then he re-hooked the chain to his wrist, threw him two cushions, pushed a chamber pot close to him, and said, "You will sleep there. And whenever I have questions you will answer them."

Dare nodded.

"If I wake in the night and ask you a question, you will wake to answer it. Is that clear?"

"Yes."

"And I'm tired of you speaking to me as if I am a commoner. You are to address me as Lord, Lord Viceroy, or Lord Brandon. Is that clear?"

"Yes."

"Yes, what?"

"Yes, Lord Brandon."

*

Dare slept fitfully. Though it was still early, Lord Brandon had appeared tired, and he called the servants to undress him for bed.

Dare did not get to change clothes.

For hours, Dare lay upon the cushions on the floor and stared at the night sky through the glass balcony doors. Though the rooms were spacious, it was a hot night. Dare felt sweat drip down his back.

He could see in the dimness through the open door the shape of the bed in the next room, and the shadowy curve of the man in that bed. He could have been left under guard in his own room—in Darius's room. But Lord Brandon was a man who enjoyed control. He wanted Dare under his hand day and night. He wanted him controlled.

Dare wondered what this man had done to his uncle the king to gain his position after being sent away for so many years. The king had been harsh, paranoid and angry. He'd wanted war. How had Brandon come into the kingdom and manipulated his way onto the council? How had he so quickly become the king's right hand?

The king must have been desperate for aid. He'd allowed his nephew back into the fold only to set himself up to be Brandon's victim. His wild paranoia had been validated. His worst nightmares had come true.

Darius had hated his father. Dare had had no opinion on the matters of kings, but had obeyed the man like he would have a father. An unloving father, yes, but still the man in charge. Dare had never hated him the way Darius had. Still, the king had turned on him thinking him a traitor and tried to kill him. He'd defended himself, but he had not wanted the king to die. That had not been the plan.

He gave a heavy sigh and turned to face the wall, closing his eyes and willing himself to sleep. But his mind

150

would not stop worrying. He missed Mal terribly. And with no future in sight, his body rebelled with nearly unbearable tension.

He forced himself to focus inwardly, to picture Mal's face and recall details: every twist of golden hair, every curve of eyelash. The angles of his cheekbones, the arch of his neck.

There were so many things to love about Mal's body, too. The height of him that accentuated his leanness, how feline his musculature was. His chest tapered to a trim waist and flat stomach. The way Mal's bellybutton puckered outward. And the tightness of the yellow curls at the base of his cock.

But what he loved most was Mal's heart. He would be forced to say things against that in court. His chest heaved at the thought.

Finally, he dozed, the smart brightness of Mal's smile following him into surface dreaming.

*

A swishing sound woke him. The room was darker now, cooler as the hours of night grew deep. The sweat on Dare's back had dried. His scars itched.

He curled tighter into himself. The sound came again.

Dare jerked as he remembered where he was. The king's chambers. Now home to Brookfall's new viceroy.

He came fully alert. His ears listened for the sound again. When he didn't hear it, he slowly turned on his cushion so he was facing the room.

At first all he saw was blackness filled with light shades of black. The shapes of the furniture, the dark gleam of windows with the curtains, like long ghosts tied up and dangling, pulled aside. There was the faint scent of sweat on the air, its salty tang.

The fine hairs on his arms stood up. He took a chance and swiftly glanced toward the bedroom. His heart nearly retracted in on itself.

Lord Brandon stood in the door frame, back-lit by the wide window of that smaller room. He was naked. His hand moved at his groin, back and forth. That was the sound. The swish of skin on skin.

Dare winced; his entire body tensed. He backed his ass toward the wall. Slow. Silent. Muffling his chain against the pillows. Hoping his movement did not catch the viceroy's attention.

Brandon seemed not to notice him. He stood tall, firm. His body looked formed from darkness itself. His hair had come loose from its low-neck clasp and swayed in tendrils about his head.

It was the strangest sight. Too dim to see many details, although Dare could see the moving hand, a ball of black against black. Every once in a while there was a flicker, at Brandon's middle, as if one of the many rings he wore caught a glimmer of starlight.

Swish. Swish.

Then he heard a whisper. "Yes, Father. I know they are animals."

Dare curled his head down tight, chin to chest, and strained to listen, his eyes wide in the darkness.

Another whisper. "Yes, Father. They all deserve this. No better than the pigs."

Then, after a while, another. "I can't, Father. It won't come out."

Later, "Yes, they deserve this punishment. Yes, Father, my seed will cleanse these servant tramps and thieves."

Dare could not breathe. What was happening?

The swishing sound stopped. And the whispers.

Dare could see Brandon standing still as death in the doorway. He held his breath.

Then, as if all the air had been let from the room, something seemed to pop. The nightmare broke. The pall lifted.

Brandon strode forward so fast, Dare had no time to react, or even blink. Before he knew it, the naked man was in front of him, reaching down.

Dare noticed a strange detail. At his groin, Brandon was flaccid, not hard. His lowered hand bumped Dare's face and felt its way upward, clasping the hair at the top of Dare's head. Brandon pulled him up fast.

Dare gave a muffled cry.

Then Brandon reached out with his other hand and wiped his free palm on either side of Dare's face, grazing his cheeks. Dare expected to feel dampness. The sticky seed of a human male. Instead, the hands were dry. There was nothing. Just skin against skin.

"You deserve to be covered in semen and shit. You deserve to be less than the filth at the bottom of a chamber pot!" came the low voice.

Dare gulped hard. He looked into the viceroy's face. Saw that his eyes were rolled up showing only the whites. Saw that there was drool on the edges of his lips.

"Lord Brandon," Dare said, voice shuddering, but firm. Loud. "Lord Brandon. Wake up!"

The grip on his hair loosened. The man's breathing, which had been fast and shallow, slowed.

Brandon let go of Dare's hair, turned away slowly, and walked, soundless, back to the bed. He climbed into it, turned onto his side, and lay still.

*

The sun rose red in the windows. The long shadows across the floor turned purple and gold.

Through the beautiful dawn Brandon never stirred.

Dare had barely slept. He watched the natural beauty of the world before him and pretended he was far away on a distant mountain with nothing but silence and the glistening sunrise before him.

He kept wondering how things could be so beautiful and terrible at the same time. How innocent babies, and little girls and boys with wide eyes and golden faces upturned in total trust to their elders, could become such hollow shells, afraid and mean and tormented. How they could turn into monsters from withheld love, or improper love, or no love at all.

He was not ready for another Darius.

Brandon might have nightmares. But so what? Didn't everyone? Brandon had killed. Darius had not gone that far. With Darius, Dare had felt empathy sometimes, even underneath all his disgust for the spoiled prince. But with Lord Brandon, he felt only a cold regard.

His single glimpse last night into Brandon's madness changed nothing. The boy that had been Brandon had, at some point, become a hollowed out version of himself. Not real anymore, but powerful enough to do damage.

Dare tried to see the good in everything. But this time he was done.

This man was a monster. And Dare's life was forfeit to him.

Chapter Eighteen

When Lord Brandon rose, the servants came immediately to bathe and dress him. Dare, chained by the wall, waited to be released and allowed to wash and see to his needs.

Once Brandon was dressed, and breakfast brought to his room, he ordered the guard to see to Dare's needs, allowing him to use the water closet and clean up. There was no sign that Brandon remembered anything that happened in the night.

Then he did a very strange thing. He invited Dare to breakfast with him.

The food was hot, fresh and flavorful. Dare was allowed to eat as much as he wanted. Payback, however, meant answering more uncomfortable questions.

"What is the king of Shastan like?"

Dare gave vague answers while trying the best he could to say what Brandon wanted to hear. The next two days were going to be rough. He wanted things to go as smoothly as possible.

Brandon also asked inappropriate personal questions.

"Do the king and queen of Shastan have a close relationship?"

"Is it true the dungeon-master of Shastan fucks his prisoners in court in front of the king?"

"Is it true the prince uses his servants of both genders for sex?"

Darius noted the repeating theme of fucking. Brandon was one screwed up guy.

Brandon left for meetings, but returned in a few hours. He let Dare off his chain again to sit at the table. He had loose parchments of notes. And a quill.

"You killed the king in self-defense," he began.

Dare stared at him.

"Say it."

"I killed the king in self-defense."

"The court will believe this since you have the bruises on your throat to prove it."

Dare gave a small sigh and nodded.

Brandon said, "Show some respect, servant! I saved your life. And now I'm saving it again."

All to further your own goals, thought Dare. None of this was for his benefit.

They talked into the afternoon. Mostly Brandon talked, telling Dare about how the proceedings would go, and everything that would be required of him.

The trial would be expected to last several hours. Brandon himself would testify as to what he saw in the royal pavilion when the guards were busy fighting the enemy. There were no other witnesses except for Dare himself.

Since the staff of the castle was all new, there would be no character witnesses. Courtiers who knew the king and prince from the past were not required to testify, and none had come forward.

Dare knew why. Any who might have expressed knowledge of Prince Darius personally had been murdered or sent away. The castle was still probably being purged of anything or anyone associated with the past regime.

It was clear the king's guard backed Lord Brandon as Viceroy without question. He must have been planning this for some time, possibly even before Darius and Dare had left the castle for their fateful trip to the Royal Chalet.

"You planned all this for months, maybe even years, didn't you?" Dare said.

Brandon looked as if he hadn't heard the question, busying himself with the parchments. After a long silence, he looked up. "My uncle dishonored my family."

Dare folded his hands together on the tabletop.

"We were sent to Barth," said Brandon, as though Dare had asked him a question. "My mother was pregnant with her tenth child. I was not yet twenty-one."

Dare did not want to know this story. He didn't care anymore. The world was an ugly place if you were Lord Brandon, or Prince Darius, or the king of Brookfall. He already knew that.

But he could not close his ears and Lord Brandon's voice kept talking. His mother died en route. The tenth child, torn from her dead body, had survived a day after her death. On and on he droned with horror after horror.

Brandon's father, the king's brother, vowed revenge. He taught this to his daughters and sons. He talked of nothing else for their entire lives.

Dare thought back on Brandon's middle-of-the-night sleepwalking. The strange words Brandon had said, all spoken to his father. All about a sort of twisted idea of power, a sadism toward those of lesser status, and a need to feel vindicated against a world he felt had betrayed him.

There had to be a name for such madness. Dare didn't know the word. But this family had been cursed by this disease of the mind. Brookfall was doomed to be ruled by mad kings.

The end of the story was not pretty. By then, four of Brandon's brothers had died in brawls, and three of his sisters had died in unwed childbirth, in abject shame, leaving bastard orphans behind which Brandon's father would not accept.

There was one more brother.

"Do you wonder, now that my story is done, what became of my last living brother?" asked Brandon.

"No."

Brandon laughed without smiling. "You should ask me. I think you might want to know."

Dare shook his head. He wanted to know nothing.

"He came with me to Brookfall to ask for the king's acceptance and to pledge himself to the king for life."

Dare frowned. "Is that what you did? After we left? Come to pledge yourselves to the king during wartime?"

"It is."

"Knowing he was alone and advised by a weak council?"

"Yes."

Dare sighed.

"Have you guessed who it is yet?"

Dare shook his head.

"You've met him by name. He and I are close. He is very loyal."

Dare closed his eyes. He did not want to hear it.

"His name is Andrus, and he is the guard in charge of you. For now."

The one guard Dare had thought to get to know by name. The one who showed him the most lenience, and the least emotion. Should he have known? No. The brothers did not look a thing a like.

But he might have guessed. Andrus had been the only guard allowed in the same room with them during their candid discussions of Dare's true identity and Brandon's twisted plans.

But was Andrus aware that neither Mal nor Dare had killed the king? When he'd seen Mal bloody with the knife cuts, he had to have suspected Mal could be a victim. But maybe not. Or maybe he didn't care. Andrus had backed his own brother from that moment all the way without question. Had he been in on the plan to murder the king?

"I think you liked him. And now, maybe, you are changing your mind?" Brandon's gaze gleamed.

"Why would I have liked him?" asked Dare. "Like you, he kept me chained, in manacles."

"Don't tell me you've never used manacles before yourself. In bed play, for example."

Dare had promised himself he would not let Brandon's digs get to him. But he could not stop the flush that rose to his cheeks.

"Ah," Brandon said, as if proud. "I see I have hit upon something."

"You have not hit on anything," Dare countered.

"Perhaps not something you have done, exactly, but might like to pursue in the future?"

Dare remained silent.

Brandon said, "All right. Back to the topic of tomorrow. For your trial, where all will hear your confession of murdering the king, you will present yourself professionally. In the public mind, you are, after all, a prince in the public mind. You will not be silent when asked questions. You will present your self-defense story, and I will listen. I will ask you questions which you must answer. You are accused not only of regicide, but collusion. So for me to be lenient with you, you must be convincing. Do you understand?"

Jaw tight, Dare nodded.

"In the throne room, a nod will not be sufficient. Do you understand?"

"Yes."

"Yes, what?"

"Yes, Lord Brandon."

Brandon raised a single eyebrow. "If you wish me to spare your life, this must be played well. It must be the best you've ever played your role. If you fail in that regard, it might not set well publicly if I do not produce your head for display in the courtyard."

Dare's whole body tensed. He did not wish to die. He had made a deal.

"Never forget," Brandon added. "I own you."

*

Dare had never witnessed a trial held before the king. He and Darius were kept away from politics for most of their lives.

When they got old enough to be allowed to attend more adult events, Darius locked himself away, refusing to be received at banquets, tribunals, or royal addresses. Unless the prince's presence was required, Dare stayed locked away with him. Otherwise, Dare impersonated the prince to attend public functions. But he had never managed to attend a trial.

It would be unpleasant at best, and that itself made him nervous. He tried to think of how Mal was free now. That Mal would be all right, and best of all, alive. That made every painful step he took worth it. Dare would endure anything to be sure that Mal was all right.

For the rest of the day, Lord Brandon stayed away from the king's chamber. Andrus chained Dare to the floor again. He had food and water and a chamber pot. The cushions were soft.

He was off his normal sleep schedule, and emotionally and physically exhausted. Finally, he fell asleep in the later afternoon. If he dreamed, it was only of darkness.

He woke when he felt something push against his side. He turned and saw Andrus. The toe of his black boot came forward again, kicking Dare in the ribs.

"Wake," grumbled Andrus. "The servants will come shortly. You're to bathe as there won't be much time in the morning."

Dare sat up.

"You are to have dinner here alone," Andrus told him. "The viceroy will be in later."

Dare looked up at Andrus, studying his form, looking for any resemblance between him and Brandon. Andrus was the larger brother and much more heavily muscled. He had chiseled features and dark eyes, but from there the resemblance ended. Andrus was blond. His skin fairer.

Dare could not tell Andrus's age. He had a not-unpleasant face, except for a three inch scar on the left side of his jaw. It had to be an old scar. The line was thin, the flesh around it unmarred.

"Why are you looking at me? Hold out your wrist so I can undo the lock."

Dare held his hand up. Andrus's nose was bigger than Brandon's, his mouth a different shape.

"I'll give you a smack if you don't quit staring."

"Are you really brothers?" Dare asked.

Andrus said, "Who told you that?"

"Lord Brandon told me." He waited for Andrus to deny it. When he didn't, Dare asked, "Are you younger or older?"

"One year older."

"And you're not the one making the claim to the throne?"

"I am a guard. I was trained as a guard."

"So?"

"Our father chose Brandon for this task. Not me. On his deathbed, he left us with orders. Now get up. I don't want to have to tell you twice."

The servants had come into the rooms and began preparing the bath for Dare. The water closet was too small, so they set everything up as they would for the king—or the acting viceroy—by the front window that looked out over the mountains.

There was a privacy screen there, which had been moved from in front of the great, royal closet. Andrus escorted him to it and ordered him to disrobe.

Dare must play the prince's role for all, including the servants, and so they catered to his every move. They helped him take off his clothing, laid out fresh towels, scented oils, and jugs of clean, warm water for the rinse.

Already, Dare smelled lavender in the hot water as the bath itself was prepared in a large, porcelain tub that had to

161

have cost a fortune. Even Prince Darius never bathed in a tub like this one.

As his clothes were set aside, Dare continued to study Andrus, who glared at the attention.

"It was your father who planned this coup, then. To take the throne in revenge for his brother sending him away."

"You talk too much." Andrus turned away until he was in profile as Dare entered the warm bath water.

"How many years was this planned in advance?" asked Dare.

"None of your business. And you will not speak of any of this in front of the servants."

"They are loyal, are they not?" He looked at them. They kept working, pretending they heard nothing.

Andrus did not reply.

The smooth sides of the tub were slippery. A male servant took up a cloth and began soaping Dare's shoulders.

"Why were you not chosen as heir?"

Grumbling. "*None* of your business."

"I am a student of history. I never learned any of this about my relatives before."

Andrus grimaced. He could not argue in front of the servants that Dare was not blood kin. All he said was, "The viceroy will not care if you show up tomorrow with *more* bruises."

"I was only curious."

"Curiosity makes men dead."

"For what it's worth, I think it was wrong of the king to send his family away from Brookfall," said Dare.

Although, if everyone in the family had the strain for madness, perhaps it had been the wisest of all political maneuvers for a king who could not trust his own brother. At that time, Darius would have just been born. The king had a new son to protect. An heir. It made sense to send away anyone he perceived as a threat.

"Anyway," Dare said, as the servants worked over his body with soft cloths and soaps. "I think this makes us cousins."

Andrus merely shook his head and looked disgusted.

Dare was not finished. "And *cousin*, I am truly sorry for what happened to you. To your family. Your mother. All of them."

In profile, Andrus's throat bobbed as he swallowed. So, that man wasn't as cold as he pretended. He had emotion. As did every human. Even Brandon, as hollow as he was, was haunted in the night by the child who lived within, who did not like what his father was making him into. And who had obviously suffered abuse.

It was too late for all of that now. But for Dare, trying to create a connection with a guard was all he could think to do to try to make this nightmare a less dark shade of black. Even if he had to pretend the people around him who wanted to see him suffer might be human, it comforted him.

Suddenly, Andrus loomed over him. The servants backed off. The water in the tub sloshed. Dare sat up very straight.

Andrus leaned close to Dare's ear, a whisper the servants would not understand even if they managed to overhear it. "You are not my cousin!"

Dare's chest tightened, but he thought instantly of Mal. And of the deal he was still making to keep him safe.

He looked up at Andrus and forced his voice to remain level. "By order of the Lord Viceroy, I am now."

Andrus frowned. "You will not be playing these games once you are thrown into the dungeon. No one will care about you anymore. You will be forgotten. All titles stripped from you. Any claims."

"I know," Dare said softly. *Mal. It was all for Mal.*

"Well, don't you forget it!" Andrus's teeth were gritted.

"And don't you forget that you are the eldest, and legally the rightful heir. You know that, don't you?"

163

Andrus huffed and walked away, staring out the window to the dark mountain range where phantom-shaped clouds misted the topmost peaks.

Kingdoms fell apart. It happened. As much as Dare felt a childhood loyalty to Brookfall, now he planned to spend the rest of his life planting every seed of dissent he could.

He would get through the trial, confess to self-defense, and wait for Brandon to keep his word and not sentence him to death. He would play the part of the prince, innocent but also insulted, and hope for the best. After that he had no deals with Brandon. Maybe no one would ever listen to him.

Maybe he would die of disease in a dank and dingy cell. But until then, his heart still beat. He still had a mind. He would use both combined to unsettle the foundations here, to hope for a brighter, or at least a better, change.

Chapter Nineteen

First, footsteps. Then a door clanged. Voices in the hall. Guard armor jangling. Scents of lamp oil, leather oil, the salt of male sweat.

Dare had dozed off after his lonely dinner of pheasant in lime juice, fresh vegetables, rolls with butter, chilled wine straight from the cellars, and sweet cakes with glazed icing that stuck to his fingers. A dinner fit for a prince, or a king. He barely ate any of it.

Now he sat up on his cushions where Andrus had chained him once more. The metal links rattled against the floor. He wore only a green satin robe since his bath, and it slid against his hips and pooled upon his lap.

It had been near sunset when his dinner was served. Now stars shimmered in the black sky.

"Make sure they're all accounted for. Tomorrow, put a double guard on the gates. Make sure the ones who escaped do not get through."

Brandon strode into the king's chamber.

Two oil lamps glowed in the bedroom. Most of the candles from the table in the front room had guttered. Oil sconces on the walls threw bitter orange shadows.

"Who escaped? Someone from the dungeon?" Dare asked from his dark place on the floor.

Lord Brandon stopped in the center of the room. Andrus stood at the open door. They both looked at him as if they had forgotten he'd been left in these rooms.

"Servants who once knew you," Brandon said, eyebrows narrowed.

Dare took a slow breath. They'd all been killed. Or at least most had. But this confirmed for him that some of them had escaped. The image of River in a hooded cloak in the crowds of the courtyard came back to him. He hoped she was all right.

Andrus refused to look at Dare. Or Brandon. He had a dark stain on his armor. Black. Or maybe red. Blood from more murdered servants? In this lighting, blood would look black.

Brandon turned to Andrus. "Keep the guards at full alert. Then go get cleaned up and get some sleep."

It was true that Andrus, for once in the short time Dare had known him, looked dead tired.

Brandon showed no affection for his brother. Nor was there anything but a quick-to-obey attitude from Andrus in return. But there was some loyalty. Dare remembered earlier when Andrus had said to Dare in a whispering rage, *You are not my cousin!*

Maybe it was enough in life for him to be commander of the king's army. He had trained for it. While Brandon had been groomed to take over the kingship. On their father's orders.

Or maybe Andrus simply lacked ambition.

Andrus left quickly.

Brandon stared down at Dare. "Tomorrow is your big day."

Dare's skin bristled. "Tomorrow is your big day. It's my darkest day."

"Isn't your darkest day when the prince died in your very embrace?" He crossed his arms over his chest. "Or was it a day and a half ago when you left your whore of a prince lover for the last time?"

Dare's eyes prickled in pain. No, letting Mal go had been the better day. Knowing Mal would be safe. Knowing he would be healed and live his life. That was a good day for Dare.

Brandon headed for the table and poured himself some wine. Then he sat on a chair for a while, his back to Dare, seemingly staring out the window. Silence fell over the rooms like an omen.

Dare stared past Brandon's head. The deeper hours of night faced them both. One more night of odd sleeping patterns making reality seem split. They were two enemies looking to survive, one in power, one having everything taken from him.

Candlelight made everything look beautifully faded. Outside, no sound but for the occasion screech of an owl. And, for Dare, an imagined glow like a promise of some faraway place where nightmares could not reach.

Dare tilted his head down to keep from being overwhelmed. He'd held back his emotions again and again. It would not do to lose control now. As long as he maintained his cover as the real Prince Darius, at least his life would be saved. If it ever came out he was an imposter, a mere servant, his head would be on the chopping block faster than he could blink.

He knew it would be another night of very little sleep.

*

Dare had dozed off. The scraping sound of a chair moving against tile startled him. He glanced up from his place on the floor chained to the wall.

"Don't give me any of your looks!" Brandon said. He stood, mostly in silhouette, against the window's moonlight. It seemed very late now. Only one lit candle remained in the room, bravely burning on a low wick.

Dare had his arms around his legs. He'd been resting his head on his knees. He did not look away.

Dare was tall but Brandon was taller, and he walked over to him, towering over him, his dark bangs in disarray, his hands at his sides clenched to fists.

"I swear, if you give me any disrespect or show a sour disposition, I will have you executed!"

167

"Did it occur to you that if I am to play this role properly that I would be very disgusted with you?" asked Dare. "That I might show disrespect?"

"You will be contrite. That is the reason I will give to the court for leniency, for saving your life!"

Dare forced himself to keep breathing. In. Out.

"You are mine now, and I will command your every move."

"You have made that very clear," Dare replied.

A hand came down and clasped at the shoulder of Dare's shirt, yanking him up. The chain rattled loudly against the floor and then the wall where the links swung back hard.

Dare scrambled to his feet, quick to balance.

"That right there. In your tone! You will not speak in that tone tomorrow. If you do, your life is forfeit."

Dare thought that in a fair fight he could probably take the taller man. He was wider in the shoulders, younger, quicker. But this was for Mal. To ensure his safety. To keep any further death count down, he would do anything.

He bowed his head. "Yes, Viceroy."

But it seemed his submissive stance and words were not enough. Before Dare could react, Brandon's knee came up between Dare's legs and jammed hard into his genitals.

White dots floated in his vision. He couldn't breathe for a moment. Then he fell back against the wall and his body curled into itself as he slid back down to the floor.

"I know what you're thinking," Brandon said as if from far away.

Dare rolled onto his side, bringing his knees to his chest. He saw nothing but white, then silver sparkles.

"I know what you're thinking. All the time. Never forget that. Never forget that you are nothing."

Darius had said those words to Dare when he'd been frustrated, when he wanted the illusion of control. It had been untrue. Darius never knew what Dare thought, or that his visions were about the waterfalls and freedom and a future beyond the castle grounds. Darius knew nothing of Dare's dreams. He'd never asked.

But Brandon knew. He knew all of Dare's secrets. He knew about his servant blood. And he knew about Mal.

"You hate me, but your hate is nothing. It means nothing because you understand nothing." Brandon loomed over him.

Dare could only gasp as the words fell into his mind. They were cruel words, but not untrue.

"Say it. I want to hear you say it."

Dare's tightly shut eyes opened a fraction. He was still trying to catch his breath.

"Say it!"

The hard kick to his thigh would leave a bruise by morning. He reeled. Another kick followed.

"Say it! You are nothing."

He took a deep breath. Gritted his teeth. "I am nothing."

He saw Brandon flick his hands at him as he had done the previous night when going through the motions of masturbation while sleepwalking.

Even though there was nothing in Brandon's hand then, or now, Dare flinched.

"Say it again."

"I am noth—" His voice broke.

As Dare clutched himself around the pain, he realized this night before the trial, while silent at first, and even somewhat calm, had changed to a brutal reaffirmation of power. It was his lowest moment. Lower, even, than a footstool.

Brandon gave him one more hard kick—to the ribs this time—then sauntered to his bed and reclined on top of the covers fully clothed. He never called for the servants to undress him.

The silence of the rooms returned. The single remaining candle flickered out.

Chapter Twenty

"Mind the chains. Do not let the crowd touch you. Keep them at least five feet away from the viceroy and the prince."

Andrus spoke to the guards who surrounded Dare as he walked beside the dragon sculptures that flanked the double doors.

Dare wore a shining waistcoat, a crisp white shirt with lace at the sleeves, boots polished to reflect their surroundings like black mirrors, and a ruby at this throat. He'd been coiffed and perfumed. Smoothed and brushed. His brown hair, which had grown longer in the past months that he'd been gone, rested against his shoulders, a gleaming darkness. He looked every inch the true prince of Brookfall.

The throne room was a wide area with spacious ceilings and shining columns.

When Dare entered, he again saw how changed it was. The old, dark throne had been tossed away and the new one stood in its place, simple in line with purple cushions added to it, along with tassels of gold at the arms and along the sides of the back. There were more oil lamps than Dare was used to, so that it seemed the great room burned from within with fire.

Andrus stood, an imposing force behind Dare's back. He'd been in Dare's presence since Dare woke near dawn, seeing that he was properly bathed and dressed by silent servants, showing no response to Brandon who made Dare repeat the phrase "I am nothing" before smacking him across the jaw, then leaving to have breakfast with his council.

Andrus had to have seen the bruising on Dare's ribs and thigh, but he again showed no response.

Dare breakfasted alone, with Andrus standing guard, and servants bringing the food. Dare ate nothing. He drank half a cup of tea.

He had turned to Andrus then. "I am not hungry."

"It's a waste of good food."

"Then let the servants have it," Dare replied. He searched the guard's face for any soul. Found none.

What a terrible reign this would be, he thought. These two darker brothers amidst the beauty of Brookfall. He felt tears start, but held them back.

All he allowed himself to think was that Mal would be spared. He himself would be spared, though living alone for a lifetime in the dungeons. But he would endure it. He knew he had the strength of mind for it.

He'd endured Darius, hadn't he? He'd kept his dreams alive because his mind worked that way, as if in natural survival mode it forced him only to see beauty even in darkness. It might seem naïve, but it was his way. Like those beautiful murals in the hidden tunnels at the Shastan Palace. Hidden away, yes, but those who knew they were there and had seen them kept that gift within them through memories of green forests, dancing people, furious dragons and golden unicorns.

Brookfall had nothing like that on the inside, outward or hidden. Dare learned this from an early age, from Darius's dim and troubled mind. But Brookfall's beauty came naturally; it caressed the outer lands and left its mark more pure than any painting. Brookfall could be a paradise if queen-less mad kings and sons and nephews allowed it to be.

From behind, Dare felt a hand on his back pushing him forward. He paused only because the crowd was so thick, and the guard in front of him had stopped.

Dare turned. "Andrus."

"You are not to speak," came the bored reply from the giant guard.

"I am waiting for the guards to move. Please don't push me."

That got a response. Andrus smirked. "Just go." Louder, to the other guards, he said, "Go!"

The circle around Dare moved again, through throngs of ordinary citizens and, closer to the front, parting a path through an endless line of courtiers dressed as if for a ball, all staring at him with cold, hard eyes.

Dare's inside quivered. He started to stumble again.

Andrus grabbed his arm hard, fingers pinching Dare's skin, and said, "You are a prince. Walk like one!"

Dare turned his head toward him and said, quietly, "Have you ever been so afraid you cannot walk?"

Andrus's brows narrowed. For a moment, his dark eyes glistened. Then he said, "Just hold your breath and focus. Move!"

Dare bit hard on his lower lip.

"Do not bite your lip. Head up. Show some pride."

"I have none left."

"Then pretend. It's what you do well," whispered the guard. His grip on Dare's arm softened and Dare felt it.

"Yes," Dare agreed. "Yes. I do." Andrus might have a speck of soul left somewhere inside him after all, he thought, when the fingers stopped hurting him and the man's strength became something more like support.

Brandon sat at the throne draped in a heavy purple cloak, despite the summer heat. He was not burly like his brother, but lean. He had the proud stance of a king. There could be no denying it. He was not ugly, and his demeanor appeared open and fair even though all of this was faked.

Everyone here was good at acting. Even Dare. That was what made successful kings and queens, princes and princesses. Fake it until you make it. That was what power was about, ninety percent pretense, and the other ten percent about working like a demon to back up your words. Of course, it helped if you had an army at your side to cow the crowds and turn their fear to awe.

Everything became a blur when Brandon's gaze met Dare's. He felt himself sagging, but Andrus bore his weight effortlessly, and none were the wiser that Dare could barely stand. Onlookers had to have simply thought Andrus was being vigilant in guarding the prisoner.

A herald came forward and called for silence in the court.

Dare could not hear the words, which became a buzz in his ears. All he could focus on was the herald's weird hat which had some kind of blue trim on the underside that looked crooked and clashed horribly with his red hair and red and green attire.

Through the buzz, Dare heard some words like "law", "confession", "regicide" and "patricide". He heard his name spoken a number of times. It seemed to go on forever, this speech, until finally the herald rolled up the scroll and turned to Viceroy Brandon who sat as if winter, not summer, surrounded him, and whose face was a placid set of muscle and bone giving no emotion away.

Brandon slid slightly forward in the king's throne. His gaze moved over the crowd, rested on Dare's face, then left it again as he motioned for Dare to move closer and stand beside the raised dais.

The crowd made a single sound like a gasp and a groan all in one. They could all see him now. He shuddered. Would there be anyone left who might recognize him?

But no one said a word. Dare had been kept with Darius, both boys to themselves most of their lives, and everyone who had known them had been killed on Brandon's orders in what must have been one long, hard night before they'd ever arrived at Castle Brookfall.

When Dare scanned the crowd, he saw no familiar faces. Truly, he was alone.

Now Brandon began to speak.

"It is with great grief, and the need for explanations and justice, that we are gathered here today, loyal citizens all, to hear the confessions of your prince and his part in the untimely death of your great and esteemed king, his father, and my uncle, the King Darius Alosis Letimer Kyleh the tenth. This is both a sad occasion, but also one of great triumph as we see the killer of your king--of his own father no less!-- confess to his crimes and receive just punishment."

The court went wild with hoots and hurrahs, loud clapping and stomping.

A flare of grief went through Dare. While it had not been his hand that killed the king, his presence had inspired it. He'd never wanted the king dead. He took the blame onto himself easier when he thought about it that way. First the death of Darius in his arms, and now this. But Mal was safe. He vowed to weather it all.

Brandon continued his speech. "As Viceroy of Brookfall, I will preside over the proceedings in a fair and just manner as tolerated by the rules and laws of this country. It is by coincidence that I was present during the murder of the king, and so I myself can attest to the truth of the forthcoming confession and am appointed by the Council of Brookfall as the best judge of this horrible crime. I am thereby best suited to decide a just but compassionate administration of punishment as we hear all the details and learn the context of matters between father and son, king and prince, and all that has brought us to this dreary day."

Dare stared at him. Details? He had been coached on what to say about the murder, and how to look and sound as he spoke. Brandon had not said he would have to answer questions about his relationship with the king.

A small smile appeared on Brandon's lips as he met Dare's gaze. Was this a ploy to get him to make a mistake? Would Brandon break his promise to save his life?

Dare took a deep breath as Andrus pushed him to his knees before Brandon and the throne. He half-fell with his hands still bound behind his back and his feet encumbered in loose chains.

He remembered facing King Millard in almost the same position. Guards at his back. Although it had been a rainy day back then, this day was just as bleak as he faced possible execution and no less than a lifetime in a dungeon cell.

But that past fateful day the rains had receded and the swans had flown, signifying great change. Mal had stood before him back then on the king's dais, his true advocate and love, bound to him in shared dark secrets and growing passion.

Now Mal was gone. But safe. Dare had to remember that. It was the one and only thing that mattered.

Dare bowed his head before Brandon. His hair grown long in the past months, fell forward, clean and shining but loose, curtaining the sides of his face. His excellent clothing was new and stiff. It bunched at his shoulders and elbows. The white shirt sleeves fell just past his wrists.

He felt hidden by all the masks he wore, the royal garments, the jewel at his throat, and the role he played as false prince, and now false murderer. And yet, as he knelt before all who would see him taken down, he'd never felt more exposed.

When he opened his eyes, the rug he knelt upon was all he saw, woven of fine wool and dyed the color of blood.

Blood. He had seen too much of it. If this would put and end to it all, so be it. All would be well. He would be fine no matter what. And Mal would live in peace.

"I am here to confess, my Lord," he said to the floor.

"Louder. So all can hear," ordered Brandon.

"I am here to confess, my Lord." Dare's voice echoed off the columns and dragon sculptures and walls. He felt the shift of the audience, and heard their breaths inhale sharply; he smelled the salt of excited sweat.

They all wanted blood. His.

"Let the prisoner rise, the Prince of Brookfall, son of King Darius the Tenth and his murderer, and face the citizens of this realm and your accusers."

Andrus jerked him up by his arm and said into his ear, "Stand straight. Chin up. Speak clear and loud. If you begin to falter, put your weight onto me. I will not let go of your arm."

Someone from the crowd shouted, "A head for a head!"

Another, "A heart for a heart."

Then a chant began. "Confess! Confess!"

Very low, Dare replied covertly to Andrus, "Thank you."

Andrus squeezed his arm as Dare stood to full height.

Andrus confused him. He supposed the guard wanted his brother to look his best, and that meant everything about Dare's ruse had to go perfectly, and yet the man appeared somewhat sad—if that was the word for it—for Dare's plight. Or maybe Dare was just imagining the things he wanted to see in his own private terror and shock.

From a footstool to this. In truth, he had not really fallen that far.

He blinked and the colors of the room came into focus. All the reds of the Brookfall guards, and the glistening greens and golds of Brandon's new court, the wealthy lords and ladies.

He saw the plainer dark blues and greens and tans of the muslins worn by middle class workers, the merchants and administrators of nearby villages, the heralds, the history-keepers, the tavern owners.

Old and young alike had come to see his fate. There was not a friendly face within the crowd.

Behind Dare, Brandon began. "And so to the charges."

Dare heard single words again out of a buzz of sound. "Assault on a royal." "Perjury." "Patricide." And finally, "The murder of the high king of Brookfall."

"We are here to determine from the assailant's confession whether this was pre-meditated, or a crime of passion. We are here to listen to his own words and judge, by my own witnessing, the truth in this horrible crime."

Dare closed his eyes, then opened them slowly. Beside him, Andrus was like a strange but steady darkness into which he was falling.

Brandon ordered Dare to be brought to the side of the throne and face the crowd.

Brandon asked him to his face, "Are you here to confess to the crime of regicide?"

"Yes," said Dare.

"And to patricide?"

"Yes," said Dare.

"And will you state here, today, that you are guilty of these crimes?"

"Yes," said Dare.

"If you can say in your own words, please, what transpired between you and the king the day you met him at the border between the kingdoms of Shastan and Brookfall?"

"Where shall I begin, Lord?" For Dare had forgotten, exactly, how to start, and Brandon's questioning was vague, leaving him on his own to succeed or flounder. If he messed it all up, he could still die.

"From the moment you walked into the king's pavilion." Lower, he added, "Loudly, for all to hear."

"The meeting was set." Dare began, as steadily as he was able. "As a hostage of Shastan I was returned to my father to maintain peace between the two realms of Brookfall and Shastan. I entered the pavilion and my father the king immediately accused me of treason for marrying the prince of Shastan.

"I informed him I did so to stop the war he wanted. This was to be a negotiation. Instead, he accused me of not being his son. Of being brainwashed by the Shastan prince and his people."

Dare turned to Brandon.

"You were there Lord Brandon. You heard his words. His anger and confusion showed how much more paranoid he'd become over the past months that I was gone."

"Was your father the king showing signs of paranoia before this?"

This was easier now. When Brandon asked the questions Dare expected, he didn't have to think. He didn't have to hesitate. It had been made clear to him what his answers would be.

"Yes. He never allowed me to attend council meetings. Our father-son meetings were private and he told me very little about politics or the state of our kingdom. I was restricted immensely in what I was and was not allowed to do within and without the castle walls."

Brandon gave a single nod. "What happened next at the border? Were you not glad to see your father after so long away?"

"Of course I was. But he did not appear glad to see me. For so long my messages to him and any communication from King Millard went unanswered I did not know what to think. Had my own father forsaken me?"

That part was the truth. Dare had wondered if Prince Darius's own father no longer cared if his own son lived or died as a hostage of Shastan.

Growing up side by side with Darius, Dare had paid attention to the relationship between father and son, seeing it as lacking any warmth, as a kind of neglect. He had never expected attention from the king for himself at all. If the king did show up in Darius's rooms, it was mostly to criticize. However, he was never cruel to Dare, and it had been the king's idea for Dare to impersonate Darius as Darius grew more temperamental and angry with the onset of adolescence.

Brandon had warned him not to speak of this aspect of the relationship between the king and his son. It would not go well for him if the populace at large knew of Darius's mental instabilities.

"Did you have a chance to ask him if he had given up on you? Or even, I shudder to think, disowned you?" Brandon asked.

"No. He would not hear any of my words. He came at me."

"He came at you? Do you mean as if to attack you?"

"Yes."

"Did he call the guard?"

"No." Another lie, for the king had called his guards. "He yelled something about treason and threw himself upon me." That part was true, at least, but not for the reasons he was saying for this tale they were spinning.

"What did the king do next?"

"He put his hands about my throat. I could not breathe."

"Did he tighten them?"

"Yes. Greatly. I tried to pry them loose but his grip was strong. You were there. Prince Malory was there. I heard you both yelling for him to stop." Contrived. "I pushed and shoved as hard as I could, moving both our bodies over the floor. A table up-ended and suddenly my hand encountered a fallen tankard. I picked it up and hit him with it at the temple. He fell back immediately, and then to the ground unmoving."

"Did he appear to be breathing?"

"You saw yourself that he was not."

"Why did Prince Malory later take the blame for this crime?"

"He confessed before I could speak, without my permission, Lord. He wanted to save me."

"Why?"

"For love."

The hushed crowd exploded with gasps.

"You claim the prince of Shastan loves you?"

"Yes."

"You allowed the enemy into your bed. Another crime, but of little consequence now in the extreme context of murder."

Dare remained silent.

"Were you and your father close?"

"No, my Lord."

"Had you ever physically fought before?"

"No, my Lord."

It was strange to look out over the crowd but not really see any of them. The unreality of his pretense had made this into a dream where no one was real. Not even the king's death seemed real to Dare.

He remembered Prince Darius's dying words. *Be me. Then you'll see how bad life really is.*

"Your reputation as an impudent and spoiled prince precedes you. What do you have to say about that?"

He saw Darius's scowling face as he ordered him about. *Footstool, pour my wine. Footstool, on your hands and knees so I can put my feet up. Footstool, come here, put your mouth right… there…*

For a moment, Dare's eyes blurred. His voice scratched at the words as he replied. "All rumors. Politics intended to sully the throne."

"So you obeyed your king's commands."

"I obeyed my father and my tutors. I made very little trouble for the king other than typical childhood tempers."

"Why, then, did he send you away earlier in the year?"

"For my own safety. He did not want his war to touch me."

"He did not wish you to fight for him as any good son of a king might command great knights and loyal soldiers?"

"As his only heir, and holding great value in perpetuating the royal line of great Darius kings, he vowed to protect me," said Dare. "He would not allow me to fight. I had some training, but not the extended training of a true soldier."

"And yet." Brandon put his hand to his chin as a ploy to thinking things through. "He forsook you when you were captured by the enemy. Why?"

Dare looked at Brandon through the rusty haze of his performance, his dream. He had no idea how to answer. They had practiced this. It had been established they would set a scene of no past strife between father and son.

"I don't know." He blinked when Brandon did not look away.

"Perhaps you have some idea. A theory."

Dare started to shake his head.

"Perhaps he did not believe you had actually lived. That the Shastans were lying about taking you as hostage."

The muscles above Dare's eyes tightened. They had never rehearsed this part. "Perhaps," Dare answered.

"Perhaps when he learned of your marriage to the enemy prince, this is why he called you a traitor when he first saw you at the border with Prince Malory of Shastan at your side."

Dare swallowed tightly.

"And so," Brandon continued. "He had every reason to attack you as a traitor to your own kingdom, your own king, and your own father."

"Every move I made was designed to keep peace, and to save lives."

"Every move you made," Brandon countered, "took you further and further away from your father, your king and your country!"

Dare inhaled sharply.

"The only reason the king did not call his guard," Brandon said, leaning forward on the throne. "Was because he wanted to execute you himself."

Dare said nothing.

"Admit it," Brandon said, voice low and calm. But the menace in it was clear. Dare was sure now that Brandon was going to go back on his word.

"Yes," Dare said softly.

"Yes, what?"

"He wanted to kill me himself."

"Not kill, but by his right as king to mete out punishment to a traitor, to execute you with his bare hands!"

"Yes," Dare replied. "It does appear that way." His heart skipped over a hollow space in his chest. Everything was falling around him, yet the colors the room, the scents, the words of Brandon on the throne continued on as if nobody noticed. As if nothing was changing right before their eyes.

"I was there," Brandon said. "I heard him claim you were not his son."

Dare closed his eyes and whispered, "He had forsaken me."

That had been part of their play, but those words were supposed to come later, after Brandon confirmed as witness that Dare, who had actually killed no one, had killed the king in self-defense.

"Yes. He had forsaken you. As a traitor. But not only that. As an insolent and misbehaved son. As a prince not fit to inherit the kingship. As a boy who never learned the meaning of being a man."

The court was restless, filled with judging whispers.

Dare opened his eyes and faced Brandon. The man looked positively ecstatic. His eyes were shining. His cheeks were tinged a soft pink. His lips rested upon a future smile that encompassed his play for absolute control. He knew he was winning. And he would have Dare's head as his final trophy.

Beside Dare, Andrus shifted. His grip on Dare's arm tightened.

Brandon stood and came down from the dais to stand next to Dare. He made a production of showing off his grace, how softly he stepped, and how gently he cupped Dare's chin in the palm of his hand.

"What am I to do? The rightful king of Brookfall wanted you dead. Executed for treason. Before he would complete his act of justice for his entire kingdom, you picked up a tankard with your free hand and you hit him in the head with it until he was dead. I saw it with my own eyes. What am I to do, Prince Darius of Brookfall? How can I show compassion for your royal blood if even your own father could not?"

Dare stood before him, the padded throne behind them with its silly tassels and violet cushions denoting a new reality. He was the imposter here, the interloper in more ways than one. Spread about the vast throne room hummed a crowd of strangers he'd never met. Strangers who blamed him, who would not leave before they saw blood.

This was never Dare's arena. If he'd thought for one moment that Brandon would allow him to live in order to show a more compassionate side to the citizens at large, he was a fool. They would not be happy until someone died. And that someone was the prince of Brookfall.

Chapter Twenty-One

Dare must have been shaking, because he felt Andrus put his other hand flat against his back.

In front of him, Brandon blazed in red, his aura spilling over in amber flame shot through with emeralds. Dare was hallucinating, perhaps. He'd only had tea for breakfast, and barely any of that. Had someone spiked it?

The entire room seemed aflame. Like some distant fire on a hill, but he felt far away from it all. He could not feel the heat.

Above him, motion. Strange transparent shapes. Pale shadows quivering. He heard distant shouts and cries from the courtyard, echoes of when Brandon's guard had taken down all the older servants and courtiers who might have known him as Dare-the-servant, Dare-the-footstool. He saw the scarlet moments of those ghosts trying to remember bones and veins as they flew about the columns and ceiling looking for remuneration.

He wanted to give a voice to the voiceless.

He did not feel dizzy or drugged. But the things he now saw—oh the things he saw. Was it mushrooms they'd put in his tea? Or powder from poppies?

Brandon became a troll, face widening, stance shortening, his features curling into many wrinkles and slackened skin. Andrus's power behind him was like the night which had leant a cold hand. If that hand was taken away Dare might just fall into utter darkness never to stop, flailing helplessly into bottomless un-light never ending.

The cries of the ghosts grew louder. But no one else in the throne room heard them. No one seemed to notice that Brandon was "other" or that darkness stood ready to invade.

Into the gleaming depths he would ride. Bloodless. Headless. For the Viceroy Brandon intended to see him dead before the day had set. He was sure of it now.

Already the void called.

Somewhere beyond the castle walls, which grew clear as glass before Dare's vision, gold-maned Mal rode a bay horse, the animal's coat a-foam with sweat. Through green meadows and past silver ribbon streams he came, hooves pounding dirt and leaves and sending hundreds of birds and insects flying up into the air to save their very lives.

Behind Mal came a dark, long shadow, ominous and glowing, as if it pursued him. It had the shape of a giant fallen banner still undulating with captured summer breezes and its own fine anti-weight. Or a snake, maybe, slithering behind him, fast-moving, chasing its prey.

Mal and the shadow moved like a fast encroaching storm. As the throne room behind him receded, Dare's mind rose up as if to escape his predicament and join Mal on the forest roads. Suddenly he could see the shadow for what it was. An army of men. Gleaming in their dark armor. Jeweled swords glinting in the midday sun. Horses running with their mouths open and their manes curved back.

It had to be ten thousand men.

As Dare turned his head the vision vanished. Troll-Brandon was staring at him. His mouth was moving but Dare could not hear what he was saying.

Automatically, Dare said, "What?"

"Can you not focus, Prince Darius?" Brandon asked. His face began to take human shape again. "Did you ever think yourself fit to be a king?"

The ghosts overhead grew thinner, but their open mouths still cried.

"Can you not hear the screams from the courtyard of all the people you killed?" Dare wanted to ask.

Brandon's face paled.

Had he said that question aloud? He had not meant to.

185

But truly, there was a sort of commotion now. Not coming from the courtyard, but from the hall beyond the throne room.

The audience in the throne room grew restless, their humming louder. Predators sensing their prey.

Were they coming for him? The executioner in his black hood and his attendant guards?

Dare heard Brandon say loudly, "There will be silence!"

Brandon didn't know about the ghosts. The viceroy couldn't see that blackness with no luminosity stood at Dare's side, that reality kept shifting the very air and light about them, that the dream, when it woke, created and destroyed simultaneously. Only Dare saw the beauty of it.

Dare had never stopped seeing the beauty in everything except death. In that arena, death conquered all, and Dare knew no escape except into the darkness beside him.

"Andrus," he said.

"You will not speak except to me!" Brandon said.

"Andrus," Dare repeated.

The large guard bent toward him.

"He never meant to spare me," said Dare, speaking the truth at last. "You will stay with me until it is over, won't you? Keep me upright. Keep me from falling when it is done."

"What?" the burly guard jerked but did not let go of Dare. "What the fuck?"

The crowd was no longer listening, and they certainly had not obeyed Brandon's command for silence. Instead, the throne room doors burst open. Guards scattered left to right. More guards ran toward the throne. They all seemed to be talking at once.

"What is the meaning of this?" Brandon demanded.

Dare tried to peer over the heads of the crowd, but saw nothing. But he overheard snippets of phrases. "...the truth of the prince..." "...another witness..." "...motive for the king's attack..."

"I should never have let that little shit go," Brandon grumbled. He turned to Dare. "The promise was you would live if *he* stayed away."

"It's Mal? Mal is here?" Dare couldn't help but ask, and now he well and truly would die.

"No," said a nearby guard. "Not the prince. Another witness."

Both Dare and Brandon turned to face the guard at the same time.

"There are no other witnesses to the regicide of King Darius," proclaimed Brandon. "I was there with Prince Darius and Prince Malory. Only the three of us were with the king."

Someone spoke loudly from the end of the room. "A witness to the dead king! Let her through. Her information is vital to the outcome of this trial for the prince of Brookfall. Let her through!"

"I deny this witness!" Brandon stood tall as he spoke.

"You have not even heard her words," said the same voice that yelled from the back of the crowd. It seemed he had reinforcements, for more angry voices joined him, each shouting, demanding the witness be heard.

Dare saw nothing but flurries of light and color in the crowd as it moved to let one person pass to the front of the room.

The witness was a graying woman well into her sixties, a servant slightly hunched from years of menial labor. She wore a plain black dress and a lightweight gray shawl.

Brandon leaned toward Dare and hissed, "What is this?"

"I don't know."

Dare did not recognize her.

Crossing his arms in front of him, Brandon said loudly, "What is the meaning of this?"

The servant bowed before him but did not kneel. When she lifted her head, her gaze sought Dare's. She gave him a small smile. "I see your mother in your eyes.

Dare startled at the comment.

"That is of no consequence to these proceedings," Brandon said.

The woman nodded once, then turned toward the crowd. Her voice came surprisingly loud as she announced, "I have information as to the true identity of the prince."

Before Andrus could react or Brandon could order her taken away, she said, "The man standing before you is not the real Prince Darius of Brookfall!"

Brandon came up alongside her. With his left hand held low, he gave a signal to Andrus to hold steady. His demeanor went from shocked outrage to officious curiosity. "What? You say this man on trial for the murder of the king of Brookfall is an imposter?"

Dare's eyes widened. Chills nearly overcame him. Only Andrus's support held him up now.

"Yes," she replied.

The court went wild. Shouting voices mingled to create a roar, the atmosphere tinged with threats.

There it was. His life was now forfeit twice.

Dare's promise to Brandon to play the prince one last time would be null and void. In the next few hours, his execution would commence in the already bloody and haunted courtyard.

Mal would be hunted—even if Brandon created a façade of peace between Shastan and Brookfall—all the days of his life. For Mal knew the truth of Brandon, and without Dare's life in Brandon's hands to keep him in check, Mal would never allow the viceroy to reign in peace. He would tell everyone the truth.

"Now, then, woman," Brandon said, voice friendly—too friendly. "What is your name?"

"I am Tallie Duran, former maid servant to the Lady Gracie Arkant who has been dead now fifteen years. She was the mother of the man standing before you. I was there at his birth and when his mother gave him the same name as the real prince of Brookfall, Darius. This is how I know him. After she died, her son, at age five, was made companion and servant to the real Prince Darius by the king of Brookfall. Her son is this man standing before you. He and the real Darius grew up side by side, like twin brothers."

"Then you are saying this man, this murderer of the king is a servant and not the king's son at all?"

She bowed her head. "No, my Lord."

"No?"

"No. I am saying this man before you is not the real prince Darius. But he is indeed a son of the king. For the Lady Arkant was the king's secret concubine, and for many years she slept in no other bed than his. I am saying the man before you is the bastard son of the king."

Dare felt his body grow cold. His head felt light and the room spun again, all greens and golds and encroaching blackness at the sides of his vision. The king of Brookfall had been his own true father, and his mother a real Lady?

The court erupted again in a cacophony of sound. The crowd seemed to grow almost angry.

"By the vows of our kingdom," Brandon said, "you are a true witness to what you are saying?"

"I am, my Lord." She said, loud enough for the entire court to hear without straining, "My Lady kept no other bed than the king's until she died. But the king did not want it known. Every morning we swept her away in secret to her own room in the castle."

The words reminded Dare of his own illicit meetings with Mal after the king of Shastan strictly forbade them to see each other.

"Where is the rest of her family?"

"Dead, my Lord. Her parents died when she was but a young woman, not yet spoken for. The king had always favored her, and allowed her to stay in the castle. Of all the old servants who knew of this affair, I am the last. I planned to retire with my secret to the grave, until I glimpsed the prince riding to the castle in chains."

Brandon pulled himself up to full height. "How could you know this is not the real Prince Darius if you retired long ago? You did not see him or his companion grow up. The prince kept to himself and did not make many public appearances."

"This is true, my Lord. But I knew my Lady would have wanted her son to be healthy and cared for. Though I was a mere servant, I was her best friend and confidant for many years.

"I saw her baby take his first breath. I held him in my arms and took care of him when she was with the king. He was like a son to me as well. When she died and he was sent to live with Prince Darius, I missed him greatly. I visited the castle through the servant's quarters many times throughout the years just to see the second Darius. He never knew I checked up on him. He never knew me. But I would know him on sight. This man standing here is the second Prince Darius, the bastard son of the king of Brookfall. I will swear upon my very life my words are true. And there is more proof. If you will look at his right wrist, he wears the silver bracelet of his month, as he has since the day she died."

Andrus moved to grasp Dare's wrist. As he raised it up, the sleeve fell back revealing the jewelry.

Brandon turned to Dare. "Is what she is saying true? Have you deceived us all?"

Dare swallowed hard. He nodded once, staring at the bracelet. It had become so much a part of him all these years, he hardly saw it or felt it anymore. But there it was. His mother's last gift to him, her last touch.

As a few yells and screams came from the crowd, Brandon held his hand up for silence.

When the room quieted, Dare said, "But I never knew who my father was. And all the stories of my mother I ever heard were that she was a mere servant."

"May I speak, my Lord?" Tallie asked.

There was a light in Brandon's eyes as he nodded.

Dare's whole body trembled.

"It is true this man never knew his true heritage. It was because the king was paranoid and never wanted the truth to be known."

"All this is entirely fascinating. Why do you think," said Brandon, "this man standing before all of us here on this day would impersonate the real prince?"

"Few knew the real Prince Darius was not a stable young man. From about the age of twelve on the king commanded this man before you, the prince's companion, to impersonate him for public functions. They looked enough alike to pass for brothers, or even twins. Only a few servants were in on this secret. I knew the servants closest to the prince and they understood my care for his companion. When I saw the second Darius dressed as the prince, acting as the prince, and questioned them, they confided in me. The public saw only the façade the king wanted them to see. Even now, the public would recognize this young man as the real prince because his is the only face they ever saw."

But other servants knew Dare. Dare remembered them. And Brandon also knew this. Any still living in the castle had all been killed. All for nothing. For now the secret was out anyway. Now Brandon had the crowd even more on his side, for not only could he continue to pretend he knew nothing about this deception, the deception itself was a crime worthy of a death penalty. Brandon's acceptance by the public as the new ruler of Brookfall was even more guaranteed.

"I never met my cousin Darius, so I never knew him. So I myself have been taken in by this maleficent ruse," said Brandon. He turned to Tallie. "Why are you coming forward now?"

"Because I thought the truth should be known. He impersonated the prince on the king's orders."

"But the king his dead, now. This will not save him from the executioner's block. In fact, you doom him to it all the more. This man you saw take his first breath. This man you claim to have cared for."

"Oh, indeed, my Lord, I do not *claim* to have cared for him. I do care for him. More than he or anyone else knows. That is why I sought out the prince of Shastan the moment he left these grounds. For the truth, Lord Viceroy. The truth he told me he himself witnessed. The rightful king of Brookfall is the second Prince Darius, for he is a true son of the venerable King Darius the Tenth, the man you yourself killed, my Lord, as witnessed by Prince Malory, as well as Prince Darius the man standing before you." Her hand raised to sweep the air. "All this is a ruse to cover your own murder of our great king."

The court seemed give one big, single gasp, followed by cries and shouts. The air stung with sound.

Dare stood frozen in place, unable to comprehend everything that was happening around him. It was all too fast. The woman before him was a stranger, yet she said she cared for him. And today was the first day he'd ever heard her name.

When the woman had spoken Mal's name, Dare's blood went from ice to fire. Mal had broken his promise. He had not gone straight home. Mal had lingered, made plans, and deliberately sent this woman to Castle Brookfall to speak during Dare's trial. It was wild and risky, just like Mal. Dare realized he could never control that man no matter how much he tried.

He was vaguely aware that Brandon's council members who had been standing in the front of the audience chamber before the throne dais, five in all, were glancing about nervously. Three immediately bent their heads together, lips moving in conference. The other two looked ready to bolt.

Lord Brandon, white-faced, held up his hand for silence. Only half the room obeyed as the hum of voices lowered but did not stop.

He said, tone raised for all to hear. "The confession has already been stated. It is too late. He has confessed to this crime. There is no un-doing his words. Would you, the court, believe the mad mutterings of an old woman or the bastard prince himself? For surely, there would be no reason for this man to lie. He killed the king. He confesses for leniency from me."

At Dare's side, Andrus's grip loosened.

Brandon turned to Dare. His dark eyes flashed. He shifted his head up, gazing over the restless crowd.

"This is obviously another ruse. The lies of a lover in his last ditch effort to save his beloved, and falsehoods delivered from the mouth of an elderly servant."

A stab of pain laced Dare's chest and abdomen. So many thoughts tangled in his mind. Anger and outrage at such secrets kept from him. Guilt over Mal's dangerous loyalty to him. And despair that he and he alone seemed to be the cause of so much strife.

And Brandon, so dark and devious, afflicted with the family curse, devoid of soul as Darius had seemed to be. He was doing more damage by the minute as he continued to speak.

"This second Prince Darius, or whoever he is, this imposter in so many ways, admits to having killed the king. How can we trust the words of a mere servant, I ask? Also, it is well-known his lover, Prince Malory, would say anything to save him."

Dare's blood flamed. There was a roar in his ears. He took an unsteady step forward, his hands bound, the leg chains ringing. Strangely, Andrus did not hold him back. "My husband! Prince Malory is my husband! And he is the truest, most honest man I know!"

"You will not speak unless I ask you a question!" Brandon commanded.

"There are too many questions here to answer all at once!"

Dare tried to calm his breathing. With some surprise, he noted Andrus was stepping back. He glanced back at the big guard and saw the man, eyebrows lowered, staring at his own brother as if he did not know him. So maybe Andrus knew Dare was an imposter, but he did not know that Brandon had actually murdered the king?

That was when Dare realized it. If he really was royalty, every man and woman in the room should be bowing to him. People were confused. He could see that now. The guard, all under Andrus's command, shifted foot to foot. Who would they back? The viceroy or a stranger who suddenly claimed innocence of the charge of regicide and had an old lady testifying he was the only living prince of Brookfall?

"You have already answered the main question as to the death of the king. He died by your hand as you confessed here, under oath today." Brandon was struggling now. His voice came on strong, but Dare heard underlying currents of shock, maybe even fear.

"An oath to a man who coerced and coached me. To a man who is the king's true murderer." Now Dare had gone too far. He'd been warned. If his words and the servant's were not believed, he would die today.

"A silver bracelet is *not* enough proof."

There was more ruckus in the gallery. Loud murmurs. Shouts. Gasps. Two heralds came in through the big double doors, hair windblown, clothing frazzled, faces filled with fear.

"An army approaches," someone yelled.

Andrus said two words. "My guards."

The old servant woman was the only one who looked serene and peaceful, head up and self-assured. Despite her

194

lower status, she had truth as her strength. Dare could see it in her gray eyes and the set of her jaw.

Andrus came up between Dare and Brandon, blocking the way between them, staring at Dare.

Brandon shot Andrus a disgusted look. "You are worthless," he mumbled.

"An army from Shastan!" one of the flustered heralds yelled. "Their banners bear the unicorn! But between each one flies a white flag of peace. Their swords are sheathed. The king's guard—ur, um—the viceroy's guard stands down."

"Why are your guards standing down?" Brandon demanded of Andrus.

Andrus let out a growl. "If the flags are white—"

"They are the enemy!" Brandon spoke low so only Dare and Andrus could hear him.

Brandon whirled to face the herald who brought the news.

"Then they are here just in time to view the execution of the murderer of my beloved cousin and ruler of all of Brookfall. The murderer, Prince Darius, the bastard son of King Darius the Tenth, shall be put to death immediately!"

Andrus gave a loud grunt, and Dare turned to see he had his hand at the hilt of his sword as he spoke. "We have yet to determine that, brother mine. A verdict has not yet been given."

"Then I give it! He has confessed. He is guilty as charged! The verdict is death!"

Dare watched the way Andrus's visage darkened, how the muscles of his eyebrows moved in rapid realization that he was as cornered as Dare. Neither man had made contingency plans that an army would come that outnumbered their guard, let alone an army approaching in peace.

Every guard under the common sun respected the white flag of truce. Andrus was in the right. His guards would not draw arms against such a contingent, and nothing he could say as commander of them would change that.

It was clear that Brandon was insane. It seemed it had not been clear to Andrus the extent of that irrationality. Until now.

Dare was about to speak. After all, he had everything to gain now. Before he could open his mouth, the old lady's voice broke through the shocked din of the throne room.

"One more thing. Dare, the prince, is the victim here. Brookfall's true and rightful ruler has been held captive, threatened and coerced. By the viceroy himself!"

Brandon swiped his arms through the air. "Take her away!"

Two guards started to obey. Shockingly, Dare saw Andrus meet their eyes and give a single shake of his head "no".

The council before them still conferred. Brandon had taken two steps back until he stood on the step up to the throne.

"This is lies," he said. "All lies. Perpetrated by the real killer to usurp my good and rightful authority, and save himself. Plus, your only witness is the prince of Shastan himself, and he is biased since he is married to the now convicted murder."

"Why would a man who knew nothing of his true royal heritage until today have a plan in advance to usurp your throne?" Tallie asked. "He would have no right to that in his own mind, believing himself to be a mere servant."

The shouts of the court grew louder.

"He has had no compunctions about impersonating a prince. He does it for his own gain. Everyone believed he was the real prince. Maybe he always knew. Do you not see this diabolical plan of his? It is plain now. He seeks to take over and has been plotting with our enemy the Shastans for months now."

This got a more positive response from the crowd, accompanied by more repeated demands that Dare be executed now.

Dare saw the council members glaring at him. He took a deep breath.

"Please!" Dare said. "All I want is peace!"

The crowd quieted, faces of hate still, but at least they were listening. "I was willing to go to the dungeon for life to keep the peace, to prevent a war. I want no more bloodshed. Hear me; I will do whatever it takes to see a prosperous realm. I do not seek the crown. I never have. But Viceroy Brandon threatened the Prince of Shastan with execution if I did not step forward to take the blame for the king's death. I knew that would start a war."

The crowd became noisy again.

Dare raised his voice. "To save my love, and to save a realm from the atrocity of war, I was perfectly willing to spend my life locked away. That is all. I did not expect this testimony from my mother's maid. I swear upon all the lands, I never knew the king was my father as well as Prince Darius's. If you want the truth of the king's death, I will speak it now."

Half the people turned away, cursing him loudly. The other half gazed with questioning eyes.

Brandon said, "His truth is made of lies. It shall not be allowed!"

One of the council members spoke up then. "You say Viceroy Brandon killed the king."

Dare nodded. "He did. In all honesty, the king had his hands around my throat and was killing me. The viceroy actually saved my life and put himself in power at the same time. A battle broke out between the Shastan and Brookfall guards. There were many deaths. The Shastan contingent retreated. The Brookfall guards quickly swore their loyalties to Lord Brandon. It is why guards were sent ahead to this castle to execute anyone who ever knew the real Prince Darius as traitors. He intended to have me continue my impersonation and take the blame for the king's death. He could not take the risk that someone might recognize me as an imposter. I did not agree to the murders, but I did agree to the later plan."

The room had become almost too quiet as he spoke. Dare imagined he could hear every indrawn breath, every muscle tightening, every heart gathering the energy to beat again. It sounded like the distant rush of a great waterfall. Or a wind tangled in the low bushes of a plain.

Brandon drew himself up against the seat of the throne, still standing. "Do you wish to continue to listen to these lies?"

A councilman, whose name Dare did not know, said, "There were many executions of traitors in the courtyard. He speaks that truth."

"Traitors to the king, and to us. To the entire realm, of course." Brandon was sounding too defensive now.

"Yes. So you say. None had trials."

"In the case of traitors," Brandon said, "the ruler in power can condemn them to death without a trial."

"That is a rule written for wartime," the councilor said.

"We had just done battle with the enemy."

"Yes," the councilor nodded. "But there had still not been any formal declaration of war. Skirmishes occur, but by themselves, in stray matters, they do not define that a country is at war."

Brandon opened his mouth to answer. Only air came out.

Chapter Twenty-Two

"Your decision, without council guidance during non-wartime, is unacceptable," said the councilor. He was dressed all in black. The only ornament he wore was the council pin in the shape of a black raven silhouetted against a full moon.

"I appointed you my council!" Brandon argued. "You were to obey me!"

"That may be so, but we still have laws to guide us even under your command. We cannot simply ignore them."

"There had been no time yet to declare a war!" Brandon protested.

"And since it has come to light that there is a second prince, his is the rightful throne unless or until he is determined unfit to sit in power."

It was Dare's turn to look stricken. His body jerked back in startlement at the councilman's words.

Andrus said, "If I had known—" Then stopped.

Dare turned to look at Andrus, hoping he would continue his thought. Then he heard a strange sound. Like a soft clattering of buckles and garments and limbs.

"What--?" Dare faced forward again.

Every person in the throne room, except all the guards under Andrus's command, had dropped to their knees. They were not looking at the throne. They were looking at him, heads bowed slightly in deference but eyes open. A few still darted their gazes at Brandon, but now even the viceroy's guard began dropping to their knees.

Andrus said again, softly, "If I had known—"

Dare did not know how to respond, but Andrus, with a look in his eyes of fear combined with dawning realization, and a firm decision said loudly for all the court to hear, "Guard! On your knees before the rightful king of Brookfall!"

Metal-clad knees clanged as they hit the floor. Some drew swords and placed them sideways in front of their knees.

Dare heard the same sound, much softer, behind him. Andrus had also knelt. He had placed his sword on the floor, hilt toward Dare, point toward himself. His head bowed so far forward it almost touched Dare's thigh. He heard a whispered plea. "Please don't kill my brother. He is broken and dangerous, but I implore you."

Dare looked up to the throne. Brandon's eyes met his. In the cold dark depths of his gaze, something like fear glittered, similar to Andrus's look but more fueled by anger. Then he, too, bent his knee and gave a wavering sigh of disgust. His body trembled. As it should. He'd just been named the true king-killer.

With that movement, Dare was the only human left standing in the huge, silent room. Only the dragon sculptures with their massive wings and bodies remained upright.

In that moment, he had no clue what to do, or say.

Luckily, the double doors opened and two guards stood, surveying the room, eyebrows raised. They looked up at Brandon, kneeling, then to Dare.

"My Lord," one said quickly "the Prince of Shastan awaits in the courtyard under the truce of the white flag. He wishes to meet with the—with the—viceroy?"

The head councilman rose. "He will meet with the rightful heir and new king of Brookfall. Bring the prince inside."

The crowd's cries and murmurs rose to fill the room.

Everything was happening too quickly. The room was a gray blur, the court a smear of silks and satins and fine jewels flashing in his eyes.

The kneeling citizens at the far end were like distant shapes on a horizon of dream. A dream Dare had never once entertained growing up, not even as he played the part of the real prince. After promising Mal he'd never reveal himself as an impersonator for Prince Darius, it had occurred to him that the future would hold more lies than he was comfortable facing. He'd made that promise in a moment of panic, but never thought to see the king of Brookfall dead, or to take his place on the throne. He had thought he would reason with the man. Play ambassador.

And never did he consider that man, the king, was also his own true father.

It made a strange sense, though, that he and Darius looked so much alike, and how the king insisted he live with his son as his companion, and made sure Dare was clothed, fed, and well-looked after.

Still, it was one old woman's word that he was a true prince. A bastard prince, but still the king's son. Yet everyone had believed her so easily. Dare realized the entire court, including the council, and maybe even the viceroy's guard themselves, had been looking for any reason to legally turn their backs on Lord Brandon. It seemed no one actually liked the king's nephew, but until now, no one saw any way to stand against him and keep their head.

Dare did not want the kingship. But he understood his responsibility to it now as these thoughts flashed like quicksilver through his mind.

The double doors opened wider beyond the bowed heads of all the people. A flash of gold hair. Armor like the sun shining indoors. Mal stood flanked by Shastan guards. He surveyed the room with a sweeping glance.

Dare's breath caught. Mal looked well, not like he'd been badly beaten only days ago.

When Mal's gaze landed on Dare, his lips parted. Even at this distance, Dare could see the startled wonder in his gold-brown eyes.

Dare said, "All rise for the Prince! Prince Malory of Shastan, you are welcome here."

The red pathway to the throne, where Brandon still knelt, was clear.

Clearly confused, Mal looked from Brandon, who remained kneeling, to Dare, then back to Brandon. He said loudly, "I see that I am welcome. And maybe a little late? Thank you—thank you, uh, King Darius?"

Mal strode forward as if he owned the room. Bred a prince, groomed to be a future king, he could not do otherwise.

Though his knees ached to bend and to show respect for Mal's status and his entry into the Brookfall court, Dare knew a king did not bow before another king—or a prince. But to see Mal now after committing himself to never seeing him again brought a pleasant tremble throughout his body. He'd be pleased to kneel for Mal in private.

Now, he remained standing with his knees locked, his hands clenched. He was still in shock. Still trying to assimilate the news that he was true royalty, that he had been a half-brother to Darius all along. That he had always been a prince in secret. Always.

Technically, that made him Lord Brandon's true cousin as well. There would be no more faking. This was the real thing.

Down the long red trail that led to the throne, Mal glided toward the front of the room. His body looked made of pure grace and style. Dare had seen him project his charisma on the throne room of Shastan, and in private, but nothing like now with such a steady, forward pace, urgent, commanding, rushing--

When he reached Dare, his hands came up and he placed his palms on either side of Dare's face. Dare realized then that Mal's great presence in the room was not for the benefit of all who stood before them, but for Dare and Dare alone.

Before Dare could say a word, Mal bent his head and touched his lips to each of Dare's cheeks before finally kissing him on the lips, mouth slightly open.

202

Dare felt the usual heat rise up inside him at the merest touch of Mal, but this time it accompanied the strangest thought.

What will the troubadours and poets write of this?

Half-afraid the court would turn on them, a mob that was still harboring great anger and mistrust, Dare pulled back. Only to see heads raised with smiles of relief, and hear whispers not of gossip or evil suggestion, but soft susurrations of approval, even pleasure.

Some minor factions still held to the old taboos against same-gender marriages, but Brookfall allowed such handfasts and marriages, as did Shastan. Dare had been more worried that the crowd would not like an enemy prince in their midst. But it seemed Mal had won them over by making his first gesture a kiss upon the cheeks and lips of their very new king.

Brandon still cowered near the throne. Both Dare and Mal turned to look upon him at the same time.

Andrus rose, a wall of muscle behind Dare.

"Orders?" Andrus asked.

Before Dare could answer, Brandon said, mouth twisted, "I go to my execution with pleasure that I will not be around to see you wreck this world and all the innocents within it."

Dare raised his eyebrows. It was strange, suddenly, being on the other side of the table now. "Execution?" he asked.

"Regicide, of course, expects such a verdict." Brandon nearly spat the words.

"Do you confess?" Dare asked.

"I confess to hitting the king on the head to get him off you. He died. So, yes."

"I have no intention of executing you," Dare said.

He could not even think it. Despite Brandon's cold and heartless tactics to gain the throne, he was a sick man. Dare had spent much of his life with a mentally sick boy. It taught him a lot about choices and anguish and how hurting others rarely gained anyone anything in the end. And never, ever pride in the action.

"Are you sure?" Mal asked quietly. Then added, "Your Highness."

Dare could not answer that question right now. He was only as sure as he could be in the moment, though moment to moment things changed. Right now, he could not have his first command as king be an execution.

To Andrus, Dare said, "Chain him and have the dungeon master see to him."

"No!" Brandon made a sudden lunge at Dare, which Andrus stopped in a heartbeat, his strong arms going around his brother, gentle but firm. "You can't! It is stipulated. You must call the executioner!"

"No," Dare said softly.

The entire court was silent, watching the scene unfold before them.

"I will not be chained like a common criminal."

"It is true, you are not common. You are indeed unique," Dare said. "But you are to be locked away. For now. That is my will, and my command." How strange to say those words for real. He was not acting now. Everything was awake, alive, unfeigned.

He had to be authentic in his every deed or he would not do justice to this day or any day in the future. He must always strive to be sincere, as he had been since childhood. He could not allow kingship to change who he was. It was all he had, in the end. The way he saw the world, the way a brook made light look liquid, or a bird created the belief of fate that could change men's minds, or how Mal had taken the shape of all the loneliness Dare had ever felt and filled up those spaces until he was brimming.

"No! You can't! This is an outrage!" Brandon cried as Andrus's guards came up to take him away. He as pulled out of his brother's arms and would be dragged into the world as nothing but a murderer, and man who could never erase the shadow of that shame. He had saved Dare's life, but Dare knew with about ninety percent surety that it had not been on purpose. Brandon had wanted the king of Brookfall dead.

"Take him out of here," Dare ordered.

The guards obeyed. Still yelling, and fighting the manacles, Brandon was dragged from the throne room.

Dare's breath came out rushed, and only then did he realize he'd been holding it in. His muscles were clenched. He had not eaten much and still felt the remains of whatever sedative had been put into his drink. By sheer will, he kept himself from fainting. Or perhaps it was adrenalin. Too much too fast.

But that sedative—

In his mind, he'd seen Mal riding for the castle full-bore, his cloak flying behind him, his hair like a beacon throwing charms back at the summer sun.

As Brandon left and the room fell silent again, Dare turned to Mal. He was dressed exactly as he had seen in his vision. Greens and golds. The essence of Mal the prince and Mal the man. So of course he would picture him that way, bright and tall, chin high, back straight even if still healing from a horrible whipping.

He must be in pain, Dare thought.

But Mal was not one to give in to such things. Even when he'd been laid up with an injured ankle, he'd never complained about the pain. Besides, boys with hot blood healed fast. Men with hot blood probably healed faster.

Dare felt dizzy but could not take his gaze away from Mal.

Softly, he heard Mal say, "Did you not think I'd come?"

Mal became a mist. Emerald and bronze. Then he vanished.

Chapter Twenty-Three

Dare felt arms about him. Heard words in his ear.

"You're fine." Mal.

"Head up." Andrus.

"Can you stand on your own?" Mal.

"I think I need to lie down." Dare heard his words come out muffled. "There was something in my tea this morning."

"A mix of poppy and valerian. You won't be sick from it," Andrus offered.

"That's fine, you can lie down," Mal said. "But not right now. Not until we get you to your rooms."

Dare felt his feet again. Concentrated until the blackness receded.

Dare saw the throne room again, and the crowd retreating out the far double doors. Already, heralds were shouting the news of a new king. Soon he would hear drums in the courtyard pronouncing it. And trumpets from the battlements and parapets, and the guard towers.

All sounds he'd never heard before in this manner, but knew to be protocol for a new king.

"I'm going to have to make a speech."

"Yes," said Mal. "Eventually."

There was a back door in the throne room that led to the king's hall. Both Mal and Andrus were leading him toward it. He could walk. Yes, he could. It was best this way. They were right. None in the court could see him on his first day being carried out. Weakness would not look good right now. If ever.

Dare leaned into Mal, but felt the big guard's strong arms also supporting him. Andrus. What to do about Andrus? This was the guard he'd first asked the name of days ago when making the ride to Castle Brookfall, not knowing then what he knew now, that Andrus was Brandon's brother.

Andrus was not innocent, as he'd allowed atrocities committed by his guard under his command, but all on the orders of Brandon. Dare was sure he had not known Brandon actually made the killing blow to the king. However, he had been loyal to his brother; that meant a lot.

Dare had a lot to think about in the coming days and wasn't sure he was prepared to handle any of it.

He wanted to walk on his own, but right now his legs seemed made of air, devoid of structure. Andrus and Mal, followed by more guards, helped him down the long, cold corridors and winding stairs to his room. The prince's room.

When the door opened and they walked through, Mal said, without turning away from Dare, "Leave us!"

"Sire." Andrus bowed. "What is your command of me?"

Dare looked up, realizing his thoughts about Andrus had not included informing the guard captain as to his fate.

"You swore loyalty to me and you are still in command of the guard, correct?"

"Yes, Your Highness."

How odd it was to be addressed as such.

"Dismiss anyone who refuses loyalty and stay at my bidding for now," Dare said. His voice sounded as if it came from far away.

"Am I to be punished?"

"For what? Loyalty? Doing your job? And you are still doing your job, are you not?" Dare squinted his eyes and Andrus's tall form became less imposing.

Andrus bowed his head again. His brow shone with sweat. His blond hair was damp at the edges forming a dark halo. Nerves. Stress. Dare had the same responses, his heart unsure how to beat anymore, his lungs feeling too full or too empty. As though he couldn't quite take air all the way in.

"I have a lot to think about in the coming days," Dare said. "I have no strength to deal with it right now. I am very unprepared. But I have only one question for you, Andrus. Are you with me or against me now?"

"With you," Andrus replied without hesitation.

"And your brother is now my prisoner. Can you accept that?"

"I—I can. Thank you for sparing him."

"For now I must trust your words, as this is as hard on me as it is on you."

Andrus stood silent, unmoving. He stared at Dare for long moments.

Finally, Mal said, "Go already!"

Andrus turned, a shuffle of cloth brushing metal, his footsteps heavy as he went from rug to smooth floor.

The door closed.

Mal still had a hand under Dare's arm. He looked about himself with quick turns of his head, body alert, mind no doubt taking everything in.

"So this is where you grew up with the mad prince?" Mal asked.

Dare took an unsteady step forward. Mal's hand fell away. The arched window overlooking the main valley flickered with summer light.

For a moment, Dare saw a younger version of himself looking out, as he always did, trying to ignore the petulant calls from within the room: *Footstool. Footstool. Come away from their. Attend me. Be my slave today. Bow for me. Bend for me. I want to put my feet up.*

How that view overlooking the varying shades of dips and hills and ranges had saved him. How the distant diamond strips of glistening liquid from the falls had called to him. His dreams of finding a life beyond this room and these castle walls, beyond the over-bearing pressure of a tyrant boy whose face was so like his but so twisted and angry and fearful all the time had now come true.

But at a cost of so much.

Dare approached the window.

Mal said, "Can you believe it now? You were always a prince. When that servant woman Tallie came to meet me outside the castle walls, I could hardly believe it myself. Others came, too. A girl who said you would know her named River."

River. Dare let out a soft breath. So, she lived.

"Then others came forward, people that Brandon failed to kill. They confirmed as much of her story as they could, that she had served your mother. That she was a proud woman not given to telling tales. And I knew. I knew it was true, and that you should be king. I only hoped I would be in time for your trial to make the truth heard."

"You sent her?" Dare turned to stare at him.

"Yes. Then I went to get my army." Mal smiled. "I told you I'd get you back."

Dare could only nod, now. Mal would have gone to the ends of both kingdoms for him.

"You deserve the king's quarters now," Mal said softly, looking around.

"No." His voice sounded muffled. "I know these rooms well and they comfort me. I want them to be mine."

"But—"

"Prince Darius died in my arms," said Dare. "He told me to go into the world and be him. But now I am myself. And as myself, I feel like—" he glanced at the bed, the open closet half as big as the main room, the table, the desk, the chair where Darius always sat when he wanted to put his feet up.

"You don't owe him, if that's what you were going to say," Mal said. He was not harsh. He had a gentle gaze as he said the words.

"I know. I wasn't going to say that. I don't want to leave him behind, if that makes any sense. He's a part of me now. He might have been a terrible companion in many ways, but he suffered as much, or maybe even more than I ever did. Do you understand?"

Slowly, Mal shook his head. "Not really. I don't have any siblings."

Dare said, "I never knew I did, either. I think the first thing I want to do as ruler now is give Prince Darius and King Darius the Tenth a double royal funeral."

Mal smiled. "You'll be seen as benevolent."

"It's not for that reason. I want this. For me. Because—they are crucial steps in getting me to this point, and they died. They died, Mal. It's too much death. I only wanted safety for both of them. Peace. I never wanted this. I never thought it would go this far—And then you found Tallie and my birthright and—and—"

Mal came toward him and put his arms around him.

Dare smelled the earthy scent of his leathers, and the sweetness underneath of that golden skin, hearth-warmed when he'd first touched it so many months ago, summery now, and still quivering with his exertion to arrive at Brookfall before Brandon's verdict on Dare.

Only days ago, Mal had been whipped, but he showed no sign of pain.

Dare said into his neck, "Your back. I don't know how you rode back here so soon with your back so torn—"

"The healer's bound me tight and used a numbing agent. They called me 'a fast healer' as well."

Dare stepped back, looking into those bright brown eyes. "I can't—I don't know how to do this."

Mal grinned. "Now that's where I can help. Truly, no one knows how to rule a realm. You learn how to act and speak and dress. All the protocols. You learn law and you learn how needy people are, and then you try to help them see how to be reliant, and if they need help with that, you have services in place for that. You try to be reasonable. You use your heart when your brain can't fix it. Sometimes you will be hated. Sometimes you will be loved. It's hard not to take all of it personally."

Dare said, "I see. Darius was afraid of all of that. He was never responsible for a thing."

"You are Brookfall's true king. You have been all along, growing up here under the shadows of royalty, as well as its luxuries."

"I still don't feel ready." His voice came in a whisper.

Mal reached out and touched his face. "That's why you're going to be good at this."

Chapter Twenty-Four

For dinner, the servants insisted on the best flatware, the cerulean plates held back for formal occasions, and the golden goblets that were said to have been a gift long ago to Brookfall from a lost realm called Winterfane, land of myths, land of fairytales for children.

They served Dare and Mal, along with Mal's captain of the guard, as well as the quickly arriving ambassadors from Shastan. They feasted on roasted duck, peaches in honey sauce, and potatoes diced so small they were almost like cream topped with garlic and melted cheese.

Dare had not eaten a full meal in over twenty-four hours. He was still light-headed and groggy from a quick nap Mal had made him take that afternoon, all the while holding him in his arms. Dare suspected Mal had slept, too, his body over-taxed and still healing from the whipping at Brandon's hand.

The food was more flavorful than Dare could ever recall growing up here in the drafty castle. Though he and Prince Darius were fed well, it had never been like this, with so many attendants, guards and glittery dishware. To be sure, food tasted different—better—from a pure gold fork; and mead from a golden chalice was swifter on the tongue, sweeter.

The food made Dare feel instantly stronger. He had not realized he'd been practically starving.

After their dinner, Dare insisted on retiring again. He was that exhausted.

Back in the prince's rooms, Dare noted that Mal's servants—and his servants, too, since he was Mal's husband—had moved several trunks into the closet, as well as Mal's green spread from his bed back at the Shastan palace, and some of the games Dare had played with him on those rainy days when Mal had been healing from a sprained ankle.

Dare turned to him. "You planned this? You had all this brought here? You planned on staying?"

"I did. I would have had my army fight for you to be king. And after, well-- You can't leave now. You have too much to do. As your husband, I'm not leaving you alone."

Dare let out a small laugh, his first in days, and threw his arms around Mal's neck. "I wasn't sure if your father would insist on having you back, or--?"

Mal breathed hot into Dare's hair. "He has many years left. He doesn't need me. He doesn't travel anymore. But for this, I think he'll make an exception. I'm sure he'll visit."

"I want him to."

Alone with Mal again, after so many days, and so many people surrounding them all this long day, Dare felt like a mere boy, not a man, not a king. A boy who had lived in the shadow of a prince, who had still loved his life and dreamed of finding a future some day. A boy still dreaming right now that none of this was real.

"Now," Mal said, "I want you. I want you with all my soul."

Dare stepped back, hands on his hips. "You have to rest your back."

"And I will." He gave Dare a sly grin. "I'll be on top."

Mal took Dare's hand in his and led him to the bed, now covered with his favorite green spread. "This bed. It doesn't give you bad memories?"

Dare shook his head. "No. When I see the bed, or touch it, or sleep in it as I did a few nights ago, I remember Darius alive. Not dying. That's how I want it."

Mal nodded. He stepped away from Dare to the side of the bed by the window, the moonlight soft in his pale hair, and began to undress.

All the servants had been sent away. It was only the two of them, as it should be. Always.

Dare disrobed quickly, watching as Mal threw off his waistcoat and shirt. He winced to see the bandages tied tightly along his chest and ribs.

"Shall I re-dress your wounds?" Dare asked.

"No. The healers did that earlier. It needs to be done once a day. They'll change the dressing again tomorrow."

Now naked, and trembling, though not from cold—it was still warm in the evening darkness—Dare jumped into the soft bed and watched as Mal finished shucking his boots and trousers, leaving them in puddles on the floor as all spoiled princes seemed to do.

Dare had a sudden urge to pick the clothing up and put it in its rightful place, on hangers and racks, in drawers or on shelves. Once, he would have done that. He glanced to the side and saw his own clothing folded neatly on a nearby chair. Darius would have made him take care of all of that before retiring to bed.

Mal, just the opposite, had not a care about strewn clothing. There was no fear in him or hint of meanness as he approached the side of the bed already aroused, his beautiful body hard and muscle-bound, lean and gleaming where it wasn't hidden by bandages.

The familiar lightning rush of excitement thrummed through Dare's veins. He reached out. Mal was there so fast he didn't see him move. Mal lay in his arms, warm and eager and like life itself had come full circle to find him.

Dare held him tight. Tighter. And suddenly everything he'd been through from the first time Darius had called him *Footstool* until now with the revelation that the king had been his true father, that he, a bastard, had still been kept close to both king and prince for reasons he could not quite understand—all of it caught up to him.

Darius's gasping death, the blood sinking into the prince's attire Dare wore that day. Being bound and led to Shastan. Meeting the shifty and suspicious Mal for the first time. Enduring, himself, the whip of Stix in the Shastan

214

dungeon. Realizing Mal was like the sun itself rising forever in his heart. And now learning he would be king, but not as an imposter this time. As himself.

All of it came crashing forward into his mind. A dream within a dream. So much death. But also, light and wings and love.

His breathing hitched, came on in a sudden series of harsh gasps.

"Hey," Mal said softly.

Dare wanted to respond, to smile, to kiss him and love him until he fell from exhaustion. But he couldn't breathe.

"Hey. Hey," Mal said again.

Then he stopped talking and all Dare could hear was his own struggle. A wind in him. A storm.

He realized his fists gripped Mal's upper arms hard. His cheek pressed to Mal's chest, the taut skin slippery above the bandages with too many tears. A lifetime's worth.

After a while, Mal leaned back and took Dare's wet face between his palms.

"You're all right. You know that. You're you now. No more secrets. It's all right. It's all righ—"

Before he finished, Dare leaned in and kissed him hard on the lips. Their mouths melded together.

Dare tasted salt from himself, but the sweeter flavor of Mal overpowered it all and now his fast breaths came not from weeping, but from loving. From passion. He wanted everything Mal had to give now, and no holding back.

Mal pushed him back into the blankets. Dare laughed into their kiss, spreading his legs and allowing Mal to nestle between his thighs. He hugged him with his arms and legs, pulling him tighter against him.

Firm warmth at their groins beat in tandem with their hearts. Their bodies moved together with just enough pressure and friction for the pleasure to begin to build.

Dare's fingers brushed lightly over the bandages all along Mal's back. Then lower, gripping his hips, then clutching where the swell of buttocks began.

Mal moved down and away before Dare could stroke further inward, teasing just the crack but no further. In seconds, Mal was between Dare's legs and suckling.

He moved his head up and down; Dare's shoulders and head fell back against the pillows. He grasped at air, then the blankets. That mouth. On his stiff cock. It was going to be over too soon.

He pushed hard at Mal's shoulders now. "I want to come with you inside me."

Mal sucked harder, then up, licking almost regretfully at Dare's bobbing cock.

"Are you all right to?" Dare asked. "Are you hurting?"

"All I feel is you. All I want is you. You make me so crazy," Mal replied.

Dare felt Mal's hands on his hips, tilting him up. Then his tongue delving deep, deeper until his entryway was slick and trembling from pleasure. Twice, he thought he would come just from being rimmed and licked.

He saw Mal's cock as Mal sat back, long and slick with arousal, and then Mal positioned himself against Dare's hole and pushed.

The familiar burn came, but soon receded as Mal pushed himself further in and began to move, wet with pre-cum and saliva.

Dare wanted all of him. This. Over and over again. Forever. He bucked up, changing the angle, quickening the pace, and felt Mal's cock hit that sensitive spot inside that made his body taut with ecstasy. Mini-explosions racked his arms and legs and back, settling low, lower, until his balls drew up so tight he couldn't stand it anymore, couldn't hold back.

He cried out. The echoing howl of his own voice could probably be heard in the courtyard, maybe all the way to the

216

nearest village. Liquid heat filled him deep inside, and Mal's cries mingled with his own.

He came into the ecstasy and went spiraling through light and shadow again and again, his pleasure peaking and tipping repeatedly. He never wanted to come down, but his body needed to breathe. He needed to fall.

He did.

Right into his lover's arms.

"Dare?"

Mal was still hunched over him, still inside him.

"Yes, Mal?"

"That was—"

"The best ever," Dare finished in a loud whoosh of air.

"I can't find words," Mal began. Slowly, he started to draw away.

"Stay in me," Dare said, grabbing his hips, pulling him in tight again. "For as long as you can. All night. Please."

Mal relaxed on top of him, chuckling softly.

Dare kissed him on the jaw, and at his throat. Letting his lips linger on the skin, sucking a little.

When Mal moved, his cock shifted delicately inside Dare. Dare gasped.

Mal chuckled again. Then he turned his head, his dark eyes staring straight into Dare's. "I'm here. I'm right here. And I'm not going anywhere this time."

Their lips touched, soft and pliant, as if to explore new territory for the first time, gentle and reverent.

Dare thought, *How did this ever happen? All this has become mine.*

The darkly moss-covered castle on the hill, the valley, the farms, the waterfalls streaming into pools of azure and tourmaline. And the man in his arms he would always turn to, always want, always love. All of it had become his. Forever.

Epilogue
(wherein minor loose strands are neatly tied up)

Every day, Dare woke still feeling like an imposter, until he realized he was just himself, Dare the bastard prince of Brookfall, now its king.

For ten days straight, funerals were held. For the old king. For Prince Darius. And for all who had died in the courtyard as traitors without a fair trial, Dare attended each and every one, presiding over them with Mal at his side.

Two weeks from the morning of the trial, coronation day dawned with low soft winds that came over the hills and flickered through the green and yellow fields.

Dare would never forget the way the rubies of the official Brookfall crown flashed their reflections in darts of red light about the walls and on the sculptures of the throne room.

The leader of the new council crowned him. The jeweled headpiece sat heavy on Dare's brow but he made no complaint. Mal stood by his right side, the only man in the room who did not kneel. He had wanted to, but Dare made him promise to remain standing. He wanted this man at his side. Always.

Two paces before him stood Andrus, captain of the guard, face stern but serene now.

Dare remembered the private conversation they'd had in the king's council room.

Andrus's head had hung low, brows nearly knotted between his eyes. "I treated you roughly," he confessed.

"I was a prisoner," Dare countered. He kept a careful eye on Andrus's hands and feet, and his face. He wanted to see if the man gave any sign that he was not now Dare's man.

When Andrus said nothing, Dare said, "You have sworn fealty to me."

"Yes."

"You did not do this under duress."

"I was in shock," came the reply. "But it was about my brother more than you. I could see all along you were harmless. Thus, the rough treatment was not necessary but done to impress my brother."

"Under his command, of course," said Dare.

"Yes."

"You have done your job, then. I need you on my side. I need you to work for me, to continue as captain of the guard. Can you? Or are you as damaged as your brother?" There. It was out. The question he really wanted an answer to.

"I saw my father castrate men who merely angered him," Andrus said. "We both saw it, Brandon and me. But it was Brandon who was threatened with it himself, and Brandon whom my father taught to do those same dark deeds to servants so he would learn power, the power of being a man."

"Are you saying Brandon was forced by his father to castrate servants?"

"At the age of fourteen. Yes."

"And you? He left you alone?"

"I was seen as merely the 'muscle' and sent to train in the arena with the sword, the knife, the bow and my bare hands. Since the age of six, I have known the texture and taste and smell of sawdust. I have broken more bones than are counted in the body, over and over. Brandon had scars you could not see and he never healed from them. He probably never will."

Dare took a deep breath. How could that experience, torturing servants, not drive a young boy mad? It did not excuse Brandon from murdering innocents in the courtyard, but it explained it to some extent.

"You made a request of me on the day your brother was arrested and I was proclaimed the king. Do you remember it?"

Andrus nodded. His eyes opened a bit wider, the depths dark. "Please don't kill my brother."

"I have made a decision on that matter. Few agree with me, including my husband. But it is done. Lord Brandon will be stripped *of all titles and wealth and spend the rest of his life in the dungeon of Brookfall. But he will live."*

Andrus's gaze darkened. He nodded once. "I understand."

"And as for you," Dare added, "you will continue as you have. I see no reason to assess any fines or punishments for your participation in aiding your brother. I do believe you had no idea your brother himself gave a killing blow to the king. I do think you believed I had committed that crime. Now, you will find me a just and fair king. I look to your strength to maintain peace, not violence. Is that understood?"

"It is."

"I am not like your father, or even the former king of Brookfall. I do not look at the world with suspicion. I am myself. I am not harsh or controlling, so I need muscle like yours around me to assure the people that my rule is strong, because I have every intention of keeping peace here. There has been enough violence, enough death. My strength is negotiation. Yours is fighting. But my word comes first. You stand at my side armed and with physical strength and power only as a last resort."

Andrus started to speak.

Dare held up his hand to stop him. "One last thing. My husband is to be afforded every courtesy and every protection you afford me. You are to treat him not as a foreigner, not as a man from a country we once hated, but as if he, too, rules here. As if he is your sovereign as well as I. Is this understood?"

"Yes, Your Highness."

That had been the extent of his reprimand of Andrus.

Now, the captain of the guard, Andrus, his blood cousin, stood before him as Dare received the crown. Andrus knelt with the rest of the crowd.

Dare could hear Mal chuckling low under his breath. Mal murmured, "Did you ever this day would come?"

"No," Dare whispered back.

"I did. Just not so soon. But I always had faith in your path."

Dare's heart warmed.

Along with Mal, Andrus accompanied Dare into the courtyard moments later, where another crowd had gathered. All knelt as he approached.

*

The End

Dear Reader:

Thank you for reading my fantasy romance.

Please consider leaving a review. Word of mouth is like gold!

If you enjoyed this, you might also enjoy subscribing to my newsletter. I put it out about six times a year to announce new books and upcoming projects, and I always have sales and freebies to offer readers both from myself and other authors I enjoy reading. If you subscribe at the link below, you can get a free copy of my book "Letters to an Android".

Happy Reading!

Wendy Rathbone

Contact links for Wendy:

Join my facebook group Wendyland:
https://www.facebook.com/groups/718074255203918/

Facebook: https://www.facebook.com/wendy.rathbone.3

Newsletter sign up (you get a free copy of the critically acclaimed "Letters to an Android"): https://www.instafreebie.com/free/3ErH0

Amazon author page: https://www.amazon.com/Wendy-Rathbone/e/B00B0O9BMS/ref=dp_byline_cont_ebooks_1

About Wendy Rathbone

The reason I write romance these days is because the overwhelming power of falling in love (which has been proven to heal even cancer) is a game-changer. It makes sad people instantly happy. It makes bleak reality look sun-warmed and friendly again.

I have written in all genres: scifi, fantasy, horror, paranormal, contemporary, erotica, romance. My poetry has won awards, publishing contracts, and was recently nominated for a Pushcart. I am a hybrid writer, publishing both indie (under my press name Eye Scry Designs) and with publishers, most recently with Dreamspinner Press.

I keep coming back to romance. Gay romance. Male/male romance. The idea of two men falling in love in a society that has winced at that sort of thing for far too long (when in ancient times and other cultures it is considered normal) is alluring. Many of my themes involve abduction, pleasure slavery, indentured servitude, imprisonment. It's like, with my writing, I'm constantly breaking out of some self-imposed cage and letting my wings unfurl until I can finally fly.

This is why I write. This is what makes me burn.

All my books are available on Kindle and paperback. So if you have the urge, go take a look. See what's on the shelf.

Love to you all!

Wendy Rathbone

THE IMPOSTER KING
(Book 2 of The Imposter Series)
Wendy Rathbone

Their love made them close. Their secret kept them closer.

Dare and Prince Malory are happily married and in love, but the secret of Dare's true identity as a mere servant threatens their romantic bliss.

Messages to the king of Brookfall go unanswered, and rumors of war unsettle both kingdoms. Until one day heralds arrive with bags of gold to ransom Dare and demand his return to Brookfall.

King Millard, Prince Malory's father, orders Dare to make the journey to see his father. But Dare is not the true heir, and if they meet, the secret he and Mal have been guarding will be revealed. Also, impersonating a royal means a death penalty offense. Worse, it could mean all-out war between their countries.

Panic. Despair. Lovers torn asunder. Personal sacrifice. More dark secrets revealed. An ending that will leave you breathless.

Also available in paperback, on Amazon, or order from your favorite bookseller.

The Imposter Prince
Book 1 in The Imposter Series
Wendy Rathbone

His love for an enemy prince threatens his very life.

Dare does not mind serving the spoiled and cruel Prince Darius. Growing up with him, Dare does everything for Darius including homework, bed play demands, and even doubling for him as the prince grows too paranoid to face even the smallest of crowds.

But everything changes in a single moment when Dare, while posing as Darius, is abducted by the enemy.

A captive in a new and hostile land, Dare meets another prince who seems just as indulged and rotten as Darius—until Dare gets to know him, until they fall in love. Against his will, Dare must continue to play the role of Prince Darius for real, or risk everything: his love, his land, and his very life.

His only chance for survival is to keep a secret from the one he loves, a secret that is also killing him.

A male/male, enemies to lovers novel of mad kings, troubled princes, abduction, fevers, cold dungeons, warm hearths, comfort, wine, and true love.

*Also available in paperback on Amazon,
or order from your favorite bookseller.*

Ganymede: Abducted by the Gods
Book 1 in "The Fantastic Immortals" Series
Wendy Rathbone

My name is Ganymede, and I have been betrayed.

Every boy my age dreams of leaving home to embark on a noble adventure, but never does any boy imagine it happening as it did to me. On the evening of my 18th naming day, when I expected no more than a chalice of wine and a few drunken flirtations to tempt my innocence, I was instead sold by my father to the god, Zeus - not because of anything particular I had ever done or said, but solely because I am considered beautiful among mortals, and my father found more value in a few gold coins than in the well-being of his youngest son.

To be honest, I never believed in the gods, but my lack of belief held no power in Olympus or on Earth. Now under Zeus's influence, I am kept drunk on ambrosia in the sun-lit halls of the immortals, alternately amazed and horrified at the power these beings hold over others, and how darkly they influence the progress of humanity itself. How very much I want to hate Zeus for kidnapping me, and yet he shows me mostly kindness, even on that fateful night when we shared a bed for the first time. Kindness, yes, but also a godly and unyielding refusal to take no for an answer... probably because he could read my ambrosia-fevered curiosity as much as my naive, inexperienced terror. He owns me, after all, just as he owns everything else, so perhaps it never occurred to him that a captive and a slave might not make the best of lovers.

Throughout my time at Olympus - who's to say how long I've been here, for time on Olympus is not the same as that on Earth - the only thing that gives me hope comes to me in dreams and visions. His name is Sable and he is a magnificent shape-shifter in the form of a giant raven. When he first spoke to me in my mind it was with a resonance unlike any I had ever known - his mind and mine sounding a single note together, a song without words, a promise of freedom, a glimpse of some distant but very real possibility of this thing we humans call Love. But now he is silent. Perhaps I dreamed his voice. Perhaps I have finally lost my mind...

ZEUS (Conquering His Heart)
Book 2 in "The Fantastic Immortals" Series
WENDY RATHBONE

When I throw the lightning and summon the thunder, it isn't always out of anger, but often from a love so all-consuming it could only be the effect of Eros himself. Yes, he is beautiful. Of course he is. How could he be otherwise, with hair the color of sunlight and white-feathered wings that drape to the floor? And he is as ancient as the myth of time itself, an immortal with powers and glamour beyond my ability to imagine. He struggles to teach me wisdom, control, strategy, yet I sit here babbling like a child, for all I can think of is how I might try - at least let me try! - to prove myself to him in some way that will cause him to crave my company and my touch, just as I crave his.

I do not yet know how to be a god, for I am only 18 and still just a silly boy who has fallen in love with Love himself, while my father Cronus plots and schemes to lock me in his dungeon and make me his slave forever.

A male/male romance.

Also available in paperback on Amazon, or order from your favorite bookseller.

227

PREY
Wendy Rathbone

When the rescued slaves were first brought on board my ship, I saw only the one. The one they called Arcana. And though I realized the others had all suffered similar fates - fearsome torture and erotic conditioning that had estranged them from whoever they had once been - I focused on the one who met my eyes with what could only be interpreted as a defiantly seductive lure, while the others held their gazes downward, at their feet, at the floor, at the past which had shaped them and undoubtedly doomed them to any sort of normal life.

Not so with Arcana. That one had no shame in whatever had happened to him. In that one blinding moment when we saw one another for the first time, I knew he was as brash as he was beautiful, and I knew without any doubt that he had chosen me - though for what dark agenda, I could not have said.

My heart went cold and silent in my chest. My throat was dry. My breathing faltered and I was forever changed.

***

We danced. Captain Mordecai and I. Not any traditional dance, but a dance of power. A battle of yin and yang, light and dark, pleasure and torment. A dangerous dance of right and wrong in a single moment caught outside the tendrils of Time.

It was easy to see the raw and sensual power in that man's gaze. But also the fear. Fear of being seen for who he was behind his carefully-constructed masks. Fear of finally surrendering to the dangerous desires he clearly felt when he looked at me, knowing my past, knowing I had been enslaved by sadistic aliens. Knowing I had not only enjoyed it, but had come to love my master. All the wrong things. So very wrong.

That was when I knew he wanted me. That was when I knew I needed him.

That was when I knew I had him exactly where we both needed him to be.

Also available in paperback on Amazon, or order from your favorite bookseller.

SCOUNDREL
Wendy Rathbone

Antares is a willing sex slave, trained in the harems of Anada since the age of 18, and owned by a wealthy master who spoils his slaves. But all that changes when Empire soldiers invade Antares' world and he is taken away from the only life he's ever known.

In a colonized galaxy where starships are as common as houseflies, and a dark Empire seeks to control thousands of civilized worlds, there are those who fall through the cracks and refuse to be conquered, including the pirate, Slate, and his crew.

Out in the darkness of the unknown, among Empire soldiers and scoundrels, will bad fates befall Antares and his fellow captive companions?

Will Slate finally find the love he's been looking for his whole life?

Can Slate and Antares ever see eye to eye?

A male/male romance to end all male/male romances!

*Also available in paperback on Amazon,
or order from your favorite bookseller.*

The Foundling
Wendy Rathbone

Diego is a powerful man with a tragic past. Out on the expansive ocean in his private yacht, he discovers a beautiful and mysterious man adrift on a raft, near death. The bond that forms between them in the aftermath of Alec's rescue is one of fierce passion, though lacking in trust. Can they make it work, or will Alec's amnesia bring forth secrets so disturbing as to tear them apart? A passionately erotic love story of desire and darkness, exquisite and explicit.

I can see his struggle between gratitude and uneasiness. He is buffeted by all things new and strange. He does not know where he is from, who he is or what happened to him. He does not know me. There has not been enough time to transition between strangers and friendship.

This isolation of his is something I can identify with, but it is also a feeling no one can help him with until or unless he gets his own life back. And his memory.

If that doesn't happen, then it will take time for him to build a new life. He is polite to me, even friendly, but even a night together during a storm with his arms wrapped tight around my waist doesn't calm the surge I see inside him, the emptiness, the loss, possibly even panic. That night may have reinforced some trust in me, but so far not enough for him to completely relax.

He seeks me out, though. That's something. He sits by me at dinner when he can have any seat of his choosing. I watch him closely when he does not realize it. At dinner the following night after we had only 'slept' together, and before we go to bed again in separate rooms, I notice everything about him, how he moves, the way the air warms when he is closer to me, the dry sheen of his lips as they part for more air when he is reacting to something, or speaking, or eating.

His hands still shake. Anyone else might not notice because he keeps them clasped into fists at his sides or, while sitting, pressed tight to his lap.

I spend another fretful night alone. I dream restlessly, wild, loud and colorful visions I cannot recall at all as soon as my eyes open. All I know is the dreams leave me unfulfilled, impatient.

The Foundling is Book 1 in
The Foundling Trilogy

Also available in the series:
None Can Hold the Dark * The Lostling: Alec's Story

SONS OF NEVERLAND
Della Van Hise

"The virtuosity shown here is only the beginning of a pyrotechnic talent unfolding into the hidden dimensions of the human and nonhuman spirit."
-Jacqueline Lichtenberg

Set against a backdrop of contemporary culture, *Sons of Neverland* explores the universal questions of love, sex and death - the three most crucial challenges every human being must face. Stefan London is a grieving man, suffering through the loss of his young daughter. When he goes to a science fiction convention in the hopes of meeting her friends, he encounters instead a young man who is dangerously seductive and undeniably magical. Lured into the night, Stefan soon discovers himself in a place where vampires are real, and the world is not at all what he has always believed, and immortality is only a deep red kiss away.

But the price of eternal life is high, and as his handsome maker warns, "Through my blood you will learn a secret which will compel you to live forever, yet a secret so sinister it will haunt you for that same eternity."

The secret will haunt you, too.

———

"This book zones on the question of immortality. However, this is not just the decadent historical immortality of the long-lived vampire, it is immortality as a change in one's perception. This is the story behind the story, delivered by characters that are hyper-real - each one loaded with symbolism. *Sons of Neverland* will have you filled, even brimming over with the sense of Mysterium Tremendum et Fascinans. Go there for a full helping of the numinous." (A Reviewer on Amazon)

Also available in paperback on Amazon, or order from your favorite bookseller.

Prince of Umberlight
Alexis Fegan Black

"If <u>Prince of Umberlight</u> doesn't rattle your cage, you're more dead than the undead!" **-Night Readers**

Thorn may be an 800 year old vampire, but he does not possess the ability to create others of his kind, and so he is cursed to fall in love with mortals, only to watch them grow old and die. Torn by grief, Thorn denounces his immortality and enters into a comatose oblivion for decades.

When he awakens, he is no longer in London, but finds himself in a world spun into being by his own desires - a world where Time and Death do not exist, a world where it is forever autumn, where the Parish of Shadows and the River of Stars become his home. It is in this world of Umberlight that he meets Atom - an interloper into his private sanctuary, but also an impudent imp who is destined to reveal to Thorn the three dangerous elements a vampire must possess in order to become a Creator.

The Art of Brutality.
Submission to Dark Desire.
Love.

Also available in paperback on Amazon, or order from your favorite bookseller.

YEAR OF THE RAM
Della Van Hise

Year of the Ram was described by one reviewer as... "A space-faring male/male romance full of love, angst, and longing."

Only after Star Commander Morgan Diego becomes an exile as a result of a Galaxy Corps political blunder does he begin to realize how much he valued the companionship of his second in command - the mysterious Lucien, an Alfarian who is more elven than human, with peculiar powers & abilities which begin to unfold as he, too, realizes what he has lost.

Separated by circumstance from his former life, Morgan is thrust into a world where he must survive by his wits. When he meets a peculiar little old man calling himself Kim Le, Morgan finds himself in a situation where he is required to master The Art - not only a form of human & extraterrestrial martial arts, but a way of living and being that will alter his life forever.

At the temple, he is introduced to his new teacher, another Alfarian who begins to steal his heart - a heart which is already promised to Lucien. Torn and conflicted, Morgan struggles with the world he left behind and the world he now inhabits.

Beginning to believe he may never again return to his ship and to the friends and loved ones he left behind, he is all the more frustrated and heartbroken when a new Master arrives at the temple: a man to whom Morgan is immediately drawn both mentally and physically, a man who is strikingly familiar... yet utterly alien.

Year of the Ram is a fully-fleshed novel, approximately 97000 words, with a focus on the love story and romance angle. Set against a science fiction milieu, it explores the infinite possibilities of the human and alien heart. Sexual content is explicit, though is not the primary focus of the novel.

For those who like a romance that forces its characters to contemplate the ecstasies and the agonies of love... you will enjoy *Year of the Ram.*

Also available in paperback on Amazon, or order from your favorite bookseller.

All of our titles are available directly from our website, on Amazon, or may be ordered from most booksellers.

Thanks for reading us!

Eye Scry Publications
A Visionary Publishing Company
www.eyescrypublications.com